IF I LET YOU GO

IF I LET YOU GO

ASHLEY DUFAULT

www.AshleyDufault.com

Thank you to my family for always encouraging my love of reading and writing, and for putting up with my stubbornness.

Special thanks to Nick for his many long nights of editing. You are my moon and my stars.

PROLOGUE

General Roclear glosses over his notebook, struggling to come to a conclusion on what to do about his former allies. He can't run, and he can't win. For his own personal ruthlessness, it's likely that he deserves whatever comes next, but he plans to fight it, taking whatever he can whenever an opportunity presents.

The night is young, but dark. Rain beats up against his cracked windowpanes, sending rivulets down onto the floor.

He snaps the notebook shut, stands from his desk, and walks over to a painting hanging above his warm, lit fireplace. The image shows a man standing at the ready, automatic pointed at his ten o'clock. The watercolor belonged to his grandfather, who always brought him to it when discussing the War, wrinkles shriveling up his forehead as he plotted out military tactics. It was as much like a magnet in bad times then as it is now.

As a boy, he never understood the implications of the world he lived in. "The air is poisonous," his mother used to teach, "and you can't even touch the water." As a General, he's learned that the stories he'd heard as a boy weren't just stories. They were true.

In August of 2025, someone planted a virus in the water supply. It took a couple of months before anyone noticed; the tumors, the wheezing, the unexplained seizures could have been caused by anything. By the time officials noted the illnesses, it was too late; their enemies had developed a potent gas, its short-term exposure resulting in genetic mutations and often death. They wasted no time in dropping it.

General Roclear has heard countless horror stories about the War, no doubt embellished over time; stories of innocent children luring weary travelers into the safety of their homes, their guardians offering a bed, rest, and food. All too often the guests became the meal. Sometimes rogue travelers were taken in and mercy killed, all because some vigilantes had it in their heads that they were doing people favors.

For over a hundred years after the gas dropped, breathing the air without protection was considered suicidal. The effects rocked shore to shore, backfiring tremendously as winds spread the virus across the globe, reducing the population to a mere fraction of what it used to be. Generations of people moved underground and stayed there, never once seeing the glory of the sun.

Subgroups formed inside each compound and unique social strata dictated how people communicated with each other. Everywhere the rich forced laborers to work like dogs until the laborers realized they didn't need their leadership, and took over. However, the workers' egos inflated like balloons, and social stratification re-emerged.

For most compounds, it's a way of life now. If an opportunity presents itself, workers can rise to the top and gain advanced privileges – become "Most Privileged."

General Roclear meanders back to his comfortable chair. So much of history has died over time, the truth replaced by many years of mis-tellings. Each compound has its own version of events.

PART ONE

1 / EDWIN

*M*y name is Edwin. That's it. Just Edwin. Nobody else in labor houses are dignified with last names; why should I have been?

My purpose in life – at the moment – is to manufacture wooden furniture and toys out of materials too difficult for machines to properly handle. The Most Privileged pay me generously compared to my peers and I sometimes find my work relaxing. Knowing that my work brings smiles to children, even painting a simple face on a wooden doll brings me great pleasure. Certainly, this position is worlds better than my last, where I broke up glass for use in weapons. It's not a bad life.

While our soldiers fight in the War, we provide their families with the things they need to stay comfortable and safe and keep our nation profitable. No job is too small to help.

Like my fellow workers, I was educated in the children's labor camps in a block of the compound called Bourney, where we learned mostly about math and basic science. The teachers there encouraged us to read books during our free time, expanding our minds however we pleased. Looking back, I think that in some way, the entertainment was a ploy to distract us from constant hunger, but books were my favorite part of school. In between stringing necklaces, a job only tasked to children because of their small hands, I'd sneak pages of fiction beneath the desk, reveling in mysteries and tales supposedly based off of reality. However, the reality of these stories was like nothing I've ever known. I was born after the War began.

Never once did I get caught shirking my duties, but others had been. Their library privileges temporarily revoked every time, I learned to be careful and evasive.

At fifteen years old, my education ended just as I'd expected it would; the Most Privileged unanimously decided that my peers and I were needed to contribute something more to our little society. Jewelry would no longer suffice. Instead, we shifted to different work units; glass, carpentry, metalwork, etc. My departure was a pleasure and a curse; the pursuit of imaginary worlds tempted me, but the world needed workers to make it even minimally functional. Without us working hard day and night, we could lose the War and any hope of rest and freedom along with it.

For years, until recently, books evaded me. The lower echelons of the Least Privileged are not allowed to read them. Frankly, they do not have the time or energy to devote to them. After I was promoted, the Most Privileged told me that I'd have access to so much more than before, including stories, as a way to say "thank you" for my loyalty. It baffles me to think of a time when people could access novels at the touch of a button, but I suppose everything is different now.

It's all there on my ID card – Least Privileged, 8 out of 10 stars, well on my way to Most Privileged. If I keep earning promotions, I'll be there in no time.

"Edwin, it's time for your morning feeding. Sit up, please," a nurse opens my compartment door. She walks up to me and gently inserts an IV. She doesn't react to my flinch. Still, I'm thankful it's her today. The others are worse.

"I heard about what you did for Wayne Meyer in the glass shop. You're very brave, fighting someone to save a guard. Look at what it got you; no more cuts, huh? Keep pulling stunts like that and I bet you'll drive up the ranks in no time," she smiles and winks.

I nod my head and stare at the steel wall in front of me.

"Would you like mint or bubblegum today?"

Lifting up my hand, I raise one finger.

"Mint it is."

The nurse wraps a loose elastic band around my head. At the end of the band is a plastic container filled with a creamy pastel-green substance. Once a week now, the nurses offer me something similar – the perks of loyalty. The scent immediately propels me to Heaven; given my condition, I'm not used to experiences like this. I become blissfully unaware of my surroundings, the smell invigorating my senses. A few minutes pass until the nurse tugs me back to the real world.

"You're ready now," she says and exits, closing the door behind her. I don't even notice that she's removed the IV.

Five minutes remain until the barred door automatically unlocks for my six AM shift. I stand and stretch, knowing that for the next fourteen hours, I will spend much of my time sitting until my legs go numb. Pacing the confines of my compartment, I meander over to the grubby sink. I still haven't gotten used to my reflection in the mirror above it.

I'd prevented Wayne Meyer from being impaled by a large piece of glass and was rewarded with some of my own. The authorities here installed it in my room as another perk, but my image only makes me depressed. I consider asking someone to take it back, but erase the thought from my mind. I should be grateful for the things I have, even if I don't want them.

At twenty, I noticed grays spreading around my temples. At first, I plucked the hairs out with my bare fingers, struggling to see them in the low light of the communal shower room, but it became clear that this habit would only lead me to soon go bald. Working in a glass shop, providing the means to end lives, was more unforgiving than merely bearing a few scrapes; by the time I hit twenty-five, my entire head had achieved a very distinguished shade of pale gray. I learned to avoid mirrors during my weekly showers, but can barely move in my little compartment without seeing this one. What strikes me most in this unwelcome mirror now are the pallor of my complexion, premature wrinkles, and the sinking skin around my eyes.

My mask smells musty. I really want to slip it off, but I can't bear to see the mangled space above my chin.

If lost youth is the price of supporting the War effort, I can only imagine the sacrifices of those physically out there fighting. The notion motivates me to push on, to use my talents to really be somebody someday.

In the midst of thought, I hear the lock click open. I gather my tattered blue jacket and ease the hardy steel door open.

The hallway fills with a sea of pearly facemasks and prematurely aged faces. Aside from the rustle of clothes and the clatter of footsteps, no one makes a sound.

As we herd each other down the hallways to our separate work stations, a man bumps into another man, accidentally nudging him into a concrete wall. Both wear identical green jackets and could pass for brothers, the only difference between them the shape and color of their eyes. In our little population of a thousand or so people, it's possible they're related, but people here do their best to pay no mind to the probability of that kind of thing.

The second man jerks his head at the first man, a fire in his unruly, dark eyes. I watch his fists clench below his sleeves. The first man narrows his eyes, perfectly mimicking his opponent. Footsteps around them slow and heads turn to look at one another as if to say *not again*.

Unrest among the Least Privileged has mounted in the last few months. There hasn't been a revolution or anything too serious, but tension among our ranks has skyrocketed. Whether it's the heat, lack of nutrients, or generations of overworked people finally snapping, some workers itch to start a war with anyone with a pulse.

Personally, I can't understand it. We produce goods in return for food and safety; for the hope of a better world. We can't brave the toxic air outside the compound or survive on our own the way our soldiers can. Anyone who rebels against the ideals of hard work is a cancer to our people and way of life.

I glance briefly at my right hand where my callused pinky finger should be, lost sparing Meyer from a quick, bloody death. As Head Guard, he reassigned himself to the carpentry unit, a more stable environment, but he hasn't shown up for an extended duty. My guess is that he's still recovering from the wounds he did sustain – mentally and physically – but some insist that he's afraid to return to work.

The Council – consisting of the seven Most Privileged – ordered his attacker to be blinded as punishment for attempted murder, but none of the workers have seen him since, either. Meyer is a member of the Council, but stirrings among workers suggest that he's merely cruel and weak. However, they forget that six other members voted, as well, and that Meyer had the authority to dispel justice immediately, yet did not.

The second man shoves his body to the left, pushing the first man into the hard, white stone of the wall. The first is all fists as he lurches at the second man, landing punches anywhere he can, even the ears. After a few blows, blood stains the man's facemask. A few people attempt to pull them apart while others simply push them forward; guards severely punish workers for tardiness.

The men are too occupied to notice the guards posted as we round the corner. I, on the other hand, notice instantly – if their towering height doesn't intimidate, their faded blue jumpers do; they symbolize their power to maim and kill. They only need Meyer's permission for the most drastic of punishments, and he always agrees.

Moving forward, three bulky guards silently part the throng of workers. By the time they reach the rowdy men, they are still rolling around on the floor. As one guard arrives at their feet, they finally realize the gravity of their situation, but it's too late. Looking hurriedly from the guard to each other with their doe eyes, they brush each other off and shake hands. The second man shrugs and smiles with his eyes.

The guard glares menacingly down at them. Turning to his right, he pretends to pivot away and plants a powerful kick in the second man's stomach. The other two guards follow suite, landing blow after blow in the workers' torsos. When the men stop wriggling under their boots, the discipline ends. The guard raises his head to the rest of us. His facemask twitches.

"Violence must end," he slurs. His voice is like gravel. "You will receive back what you give. You're all late."

A light at the end of the hallway flickers. Next to it is the entrance to the carpentry unit – so close, but not close enough.

"Your meals will all be delayed by one hour tonight. If you are sleeping when the nurse arrives, you will not receive any feeding at all for another day. Do you understand?" the voice of a second guard, not wearing a mask, carries clearly down the hallway.

"Let this be a warning," the guard spits. He turns and walks away, observing the ranks of workers as he passes.

"On your way!" the second guard hisses. He gestures at a couple of guards just standing around. "You two, bring these men to the infirmary."

The tension in the air evaporates as soon as I arrive at my workstation. Today is a painting day. Sitting on a wooden stool, I scan over the array of toys separated on the workbench. The station in front of me has been assigned mostly dolls while mine is covered with wooden tugboats, splinters poking out of the edges. I caress the brushes and small, battered cans of spray paint that lay on the table as people filter into the room. Someone sits down in front of me. I look up.

She's the most beautiful woman I've ever seen. Black hair sprouts from her ponytail and splays against her face around her eyes and mask. Her eyes are large, the vibrant color of ripe blueberries I've only seen in magazines, and strikingly present. I can't help but stare a little too long. She doesn't look young, probably hovering around thirty, yet she has somehow avoided the pesky wrinkles and grays that plague the rest of us.

She looks up and waves.

Are you new? I point to her and raise nine fingers above my head.

She nods, slowly readjusting the left ear loop of her cloth mask. She scans the workbench, hardly interested in me at all.

What's your name? I point to my head and make a talking hand.

I know that this might be a difficult question to answer. Like myself, this woman appears to have been born without a functioning mouth. Vocal chords are an issue for many of us, as well, but once in a while you meet someone capable of making an unpleasant grunting sound. The genetic lottery, leadership told us. An effect of the War. We lost.

The woman looks down at the workbench for a moment, thinking of how to answer. Then, looking back up at me with a smile in her eyes, she reaches for a pencil. Grabbing one of the dolls from her side, she begins sketching something on the bottom of a dainty shoe. She searches the room to see if anyone's watching and then hands the doll to me.

Airlee, it reads.

Interesting name. I gaze up at her for a moment. A guard will arrive in the room soon, so this conversation needs to progress quickly. I signal to her to hand me the pencil. She reaches over and accidentally touches my maimed hand, sending an electric wave through my fingers.

I scribble *Edwin* under her neatly written name and thrust the doll at her in a nervous rush. Getting caught using supplies for unapproved uses would send both of us to the infirmary, too.

She reads the doll's shoe and nods her head, bobbing her ponytail up and down. She glances at the door and smothers the head of a brush with black paint right as a guard strolls into the room. Within just a second, our names are covered with a layer of thick paint.

Meyer's Second arrives at the front of the room, exactly the last person we want to see after the display in the hallway. Then again, what must be done must be done. Someone has to sort people out.

"Attention," he says, "I will oversee your positions for the week. Meyer is still recovering from complications related to his previous posting and will be performing lighter duties than usual."

Someone taps the bottom of their workbench, pointing out

the irony in his words. Nothing about the guards' responsibilities in the carpentry shop indicate anything but light duty.

A curious young woman makes the mistake of raising her hand and tilting her head. My guess is that she wants to know exactly what's wrong with Meyer.

"Look," the guard begins, struggling to quell the acid in his voice, "I didn't choose to work with you invalids. My job was to oversee the great grapevines of the greenhouse before one of you stabbed him. Frankly, I don't care how hard you work as long as you get what you need to done. Lunch is in six hours. Get moving."

No wonder he has so much more color in his skin than the rest of us; he was transferred from Luna Bay, the compound's only greenhouse. Although most of us have never been inside, it's well known for its skylights, offering up the only source of natural light in the entire building. What I wouldn't give for a chance to become a guard, dawdling among fresh greenery and watching the clouds roll by.

Meyer used to look like us workers, born disfigured, but this guard does not. The questions make my head swirl. My guess? Genetic lottery.

The intercom squeaks on. The voice of Samuel Garley, the Head Councilor, blares through tinny speakers.

"Good morning, everyone," he begins, "and thank you for

another day of hard work. Together, I know we will conquer our enemies and take back what is ours. To accomplish our goals, we must work alongside each other in *peace* and *harmony*. Remember: those who show themselves most capable shall be rewarded. Now, please rise for the Vow."

A few workers around the room roll their eyes, but no one dares to disobey. We stand as straight as possible and thrust our hands forward as if longing for something just out of reach. In my peripheral vision, an older woman struggles with the movement; it's well known among workers that she has a tumor in her stomach, but she won't get help for it. At her age, the Most Privileged would probably euthanize her.

I wonder to myself what the pose must look like to Meyer's Second as he stands at the front of the room. He faces us as he holds the position, but stares at the wall. His cheeks redden. A handful of people in the room reach out to him, staring him directly in the eyes as they grasp forward.

Samuel's voice returns to the speaker:

"I solemnly vow to support the United Army in its effort to combat all evils, to shed all darkness, and make room for the light. No contribution is too great or too small. I vow to work at my hardest for as long as I may live, and support my brethren in their own efforts for the hope of a better tomorrow."

The room gently whooshes as we slip back into our seats.

"Remember, my friends. We do this together. Each and every day. We *will* prosper!"

* * *

Airlee finishes her tasks long before me. A perfectionist, I want to make sure these toys are ideal, painted as well as possible. I think of the young children who will play with them, roll them around in their clean little hands while seated in their warm, dry homes, waiting for their fathers or mothers to return home from battle. I try to imagine the delight in their voices, but can't. I've never heard a child's voice. Where I'm from, no one grew up with mouths.

I can feel Airlee's gaze on me, sizing my skills up, as I concentrate on the trim of a tugboat. I look up briefly, only for her to avert her gaze. The sides of her eyes droop. She looks bored.

Splinters from the tugboat's edges rise and become more prominent with every stroke. I exhale deeply from my nose. I pray that a caked-on layer of paint will cure the problem, so I attack the tugboat more aggressively.

She turns her head back in my direction and nods from behind the tugboat. I ignore her, choosing to pull out a particularly obnoxious splinter instead, only it extends deeper than I thought. Its roots take a larger strip of wood with it. Splinters feather through the blue paint, itching to be picked at. I narrow my eyes at the project.

I feel a hand on mine, urging me to stop. Airlee. She shakes her head, wrinkles emerging around her eyes. She points to me and opens her hands as if she's reading a book. *Did no one ever train you?*

I tilt my head. Is she really making fun of me?

She points to the shared toolbox at the middle of the table; it's rusted to Hell and I wouldn't be surprised if it bottomed out if lifted. Muddling through the array of ancient tools and art supplies, she seems to find what she's rummaging for. It looks thin and insubstantial. How can this possibly help me?

Airlee holds her hand out, waiting for me to accept the mysterious piece of paper. I reach out hesitantly.

It's rough. It feels almost as though tiny shards of glass, hardly existent, were glued to the sheet along with sand and dust. It's totally worn down on one side. *Charlie's Sanding* is advertised on the good side, barely even visible. I wonder if the company is still in business somewhere or if, like so many other businesses, the War swallowed it whole. I think I know what the paper is for, but have never used one of these before. The realization dawns on Airlee:

I'm relatively new, too. I'm not an expert. But she is. Apparently.

Exasperation plasters her face momentarily. She snatches the sheet back and motions for my tugboat. She presses the paper to the dry, splintered areas and rubs in small circles. I panic and practically jump over the table to pluck back the toy. Other workers look in our direction and raise their eyebrows at us. Specks of blue dust on the table mock me – so much for my hard work.

With a proud flourish, she passes the boat back along with the blue-smudged, sandy tool. I'm amazed; where I had struggled to paint is now relatively smooth – enough to paint on properly, at least.

She points at the tugboat, makes circular motions with her left hand, and nods.

I wonder how she knows so much about woodworking techniques. What was her old position?

The rest of the day continues in much the same fashion, Airlee pausing to correct my silly little mistakes. Around midday, nurses come in and administer our feedings. One of them catches me studying a large bruise developing in the crook of my elbow before she rolls my sleeve down. I register pity in the dark wells of her eyes as she finishes up with me. I try to ignore it and focus on getting back to work. Productivity is all that matters. It is what keeps us all alive.

"I don't deserve this life," she mutters as she clutches her medical bag and swiftly exits the room. I stare after her. Standing beside the door, the guard peeks down at her buttocks as soon as her back faces him.

His own lunch consists of a smooth, shiny, red apple and a sandwich of some kind. He leaves the apple half-eaten on a desk at the front of the room where it turns brown and slowly rots, but not before expressing its juicy aroma. My mouth salivates, though the saliva has no place to go but down. If I use my imagination, I can sense what an apple tastes like.

After a couple of hours, he picks up the half-eaten apple and chucks it into a short barrel on the other side of the room. He celebrates making the shot by pumping his elbow down to his hip. No one cares; no one else is watching. The scent of the fruit fades as dust and other debris pile onto it. In a brief hour, I forget what an apple even smells like.

* * *

By the end of the day, my hands ache and my eyes hurt from focusing them so close to my face for so long. Paint has seeped through layers of skin, ensuring that no basic scrub down will release the bright colors from underneath my flesh. I hide my hands in my jacket pockets as often as possible in case anyone questions me about wasting supplies.

With what little time remains before lights out, I furtively venture to the library. It's been years since I've stepped inside a place of learning; I'm not sure that I even remember how to read very well anymore. The guard at the door gives me a brief nod. He's a placid looking fellow, sleepy, but young. He's probably new; he looks worriless.

I pity many of the guards here. While we workers produce things for the world to consume, they have nothing tangible to prove their worth. Some guards, like this man, will never experience anything like what happened in the hall this morning. Their entire careers will be spent guarding the words of dead men, never seeing an opening for a promotion. Their only hope is to wait for someone above them to die – and even then, the probability is almost nil.

Frenetically, I head to the center of the room, avoiding the obstacles posed by smaller bookcases featuring thin children's stories. I look around at the gradually decaying paperbacks, yellowed pages creating a must in the air – sections for trades, a young adult department, even grade school fiction. I can't decide where to begin. Do I go for a fun story or for something more factual? What nuggets of worth do each of these books contain? I want to harness their contents and absorb them like a sponge, all at once. I have missed so many years of exploring the worlds within these pages.

My heart races. What if, by chance, a book was moved to the library that I've never seen before? Likewise, are my favorites still on the shelves?

A head bobs up behind a bookcase in the trades department. Black hair, frazzled eyes. I recognize her immediately; I spent the morning and afternoon stealing glances at these eyes. She's holding a copy of a hardcover textbook, *The Carpenter's Guide to Working with Wood.*

Good, I think, *if I can read the cover of a book, I can read the actual pages.*

The labored breathing from my clogged nose must alert her to my presence. She lifts her head with concern. I wave automatically. Aside from the ghosts of ancient plumbing authors and rambling poets who may as well speak Greek, we're alone.

Something flashes in her eyes and disappears as quickly as it came. Fear?

It takes her a moment to unfurrow her eyebrows and wave back. She snaps the book shut.

Perhaps she didn't recognize me at first. In this enormous compound, with most workers and guards sporting facemasks, it's completely plausible. Identifying someone by their eyes and communicating with them that way has become a necessity. Still, it takes a long time to really pin someone down.

I nod at her and the carpentry book, hoping that she'll understand my question without writing utensils around. *Is this how you know so much about woodwork?*

She shrugs and seesaws her hand. I have no idea if she

thinks I asked her something different, like if she actually enjoys woodwork. Like many people with access to the library, she could just be loitering in the trades section in hopes of getting a promotion. If no one on the job recognizes that you're successful, you can always pretend to be conscientious outside of work and hope someone notices.

I curse our birth defects.

"Ten minutes until close!" a perky librarian rushes into the room. The enormous stack of books in her arms begins to teeter and slip. They fall to the floor like a colossal house of cards. The loose pages of ancient novels litter the musty red carpet and *The Short Mysteries of Drugsberry* lands at my feet. I pick it up.

The novel's cover piques my curiosity. It's a painting of a man in a raincoat holding an umbrella, his head slightly cocked and back turned to the viewer. Despite the man's attire, the sky is an absolutely spotless blue. The paperback covers and the pages sandwiched within smell sickly sweet with age.

The umbrella serves as a reminder to me that I've never felt the splash of rain upon my face and probably never will. My only hope is for us to win the War and find a cure for the diseases the noxious air outside produces.

I flip the book over and read its minuscule description:

"Donald Feeny, a meek accountant who dreams of becoming the world's next biggest playwright, struggles to accept the world as it continues to reject his masterpieces. Initially convinced that his tale of an illegal Spanish-American immigrant's unlikely success will bring hope to young men aspiring for a better life, Donald's perspective evolves when he meets a mysterious man named Alderman – a devil in disguise who can hand Donald anything he desires. Will Donald resist temptation?"

"Aren't you a cerebral young man?" the librarian laughs as her restored pile of books teeters again. "Why don't you keep that one? Cut some slack on these uncoordinated arms. Bring it back in a week?"

I nod, looking from the book, to her, to Airlee.

Only Airlee has gone. In my torrent of fascination, she must have slipped through the door.

Thinking of my own time constraints, I decide that leaving isn't such a bad idea. Feeding will be delayed tonight because of the morning's ruckus. Missing a meal could make for a hard, sleepless night.

I flip through *The Short Mysteries of Drugsberry* before lights out. The description on the back cover only details the story of a man in a nine-page tale, the first of several longer short stories contained in the book's weary pages. I flip to the first page.

"Donald Feeny's fingers chip away at his prehistoric type-writer. A stack of expense reports sitting on his desk taunts him, but Feeny knows not to fear this: He is a force to be reckoned with."

The light above me blinks out. I'll have to delve into this on another day.

* * *

I wake on and off all night despite receiving the evening's meager sustenance. The damp chill of my room makes me shiver all over. Perspiration collects on my forehead and seeps into my clothes; I have been having nightmares again, thinking about the outside world of which I have seen so very little.

Typically, my dreams look the same, reoccurring once every month or so during times of particularly serious mental stress. My door unlocks, but no nurse comes to visit me. The inside of my room is all I know, memories washed away by some unknown force. Essentially born as a 25-year-old man, I venture out of the womb to explore in new, unfamiliar surroundings. Empty, echoing hallways signal to me that the building has been evacuated – or, perhaps more terrifying, never occupied by anyone other than myself at all. No guards. No workers. Pure nothingness. Little by little, I regain my memory.

Just as I begin to find peace in the compound's quietude, a shadow along the far wall steals my attention. The outline of a wide-brimmed hat elongates its head, making it seem more alien than human. I follow the mysterious man's shadow without another thought. As I reach the corner, I find that there's no one there at all.

Instead, a blazing world of white lies in front of me, waiting beyond a simple door. In the waking universe, the doors' windows have been blacked out for as long as I can remember, the door itself chained closed. In reality, the door doesn't lead anywhere particularly notable, just an abandoned room in an area of the building hardly anyone visits. In my dream, the door is a portal to a whole new universe.

Once my eyes adjust to the assault on my vision, emerald waves of grass and small yellow daisies reveal themselves through gossamers of light. I struggle through the tears that well up in my eyes and take another step forward.

It's been well over a decade since I've seen natural daylight or stepped on anything other than concrete. It saddens me to admit it, but I'm the reason children no longer go on educational trips to Luna Bay. In an overexcited fit as a kid, I plowed through a garden patch, ripping up carrots and scallions as I ran. That stunt earned me a couple of days in the Detention Center. Now, most children don't have the slightest idea what the Sun even looks like. Only the Most Privileged do.

The visage of the outdoors lures me closer like some invisible giant that's wrapped its arms around my body to haul me in. I raise my hand to shield my eyes against the Sun and walk out onto a dry patch of dirt just outside the doorway.

I remember why this is a nightmare.

Suddenly I'm watching myself from above as the lower half of my face contorts and burns. A beautiful mountain view directly in front of me demands my attention, but the pain is far more compelling. I clap the lower half of my face and touch bare, fiery skin. My mask had come off of my face at some point during my venturing.

As the burning sensation grows, an invisible knife slices at the mottled space where my lips should be. Blood drizzles down my chin and sullies the ground. My flesh boils. In a panic, I turn back to the door only to find it shut and its windows once more blacked out. I bang on it to no avail. I've been locked out. I'm not alone, after all, but my mystery companion has no sympathy for me.

A light breeze sends daggers into a four-inch slit in my face, the cuts imprecise and jagged. Even though I know it's just a dream, the pain feels so real.

As blood gushes from my face, a twisted realization washes over me; I am mouth breathing, something I have never done in my entire life. A not completely unpleasant taste enters my mouth as blood trickles against my tongue. The gash in my face exposes a set of rotten, crooked teeth that makes my stomach churn.

Then I'm no longer in control of my maimed body. The creature in front of me smiles, revealing nothing but the signs of sickness as it shows off blood-smeared teeth. The stench of its breath makes bile coat the back of my throat.

The bed rattles as I lurch awake and struggle to control breathing through my nose. My deformities give me peace. They are familiar.

2 / ZURIE

Zurie listens for the telltale signs of her husband's sleeping, then she waits a few minutes more; the sounds of his snores steady, but not yet loud enough to wake himself up. She slips out from under the covers and grabs a long jacket to cover up her bedclothes. If she bumps into someone, she'll say she can't sleep. She's on a night walk.

It's 2:30 AM and she's late for a meeting with Sanguine, the man she begrudgingly partnered up with for her mission to reshape the compound. He makes her uncomfortable during their meetings alone – he has a killer's eyes – but he wouldn't dare touch her, not with her standing. Her followers would rat him out in an instant and his whole organization would fall. As much as they hate each other, neither of them can bear to imagine the setbacks that either one of them getting caught would cause.

The ghostly light of the hallways makes her want to crawl

back into bed. She pushes her bare feet harder, her steps ultimately leading her to Sanitation. For years, she complained that it should never be left unmanned, even at night. Now, funny enough, Sanguine is watching over it.

"You're late," he says as she walks through the door. He looks like a criminal lying back against the wall, bored, his signature red bandana covering up the lower portion of his face.

"Well, it's not like you're going anywhere," she replies. She barely looks over at him, instead surveying the room first.

"You forget your shoes?" he nods at her feet, one stepping on the other for warmth. He imagines the concrete is cold, but he's never been stupid enough to go without footwear.

"I didn't want to wake my husband," she rolls her eyes. She stands still and waits for him to rise. They listen to the hum of machines as a minute passes.

He finally pushes himself up off the floor, taking his time. He dusts off his dirty uniform, reaches in his front pocket, and takes out a crumpled note. He unfolds it for her and passes it her way. Its heading reads "Weekly Evaluation Bullshit." He readjusts his bandana while she reads his report, her eyebrows raised the entire time.

"You've got to be kidding me with this, Sanguine. You mixed oil with the fertilizer? Had three guys jump a guard outside the kids' labor camp? What is any of this going to accomplish? Give me one good reason right now why I shouldn't just turn you in before you starve us all."

He stares at the ground and answers slowly. "I'm showing the Council that things aren't working here. I'm showing the U.A. that we need more help than we're getting. They've got to find the resources somewhere."

"The United Army doesn't care if our victory garden sucks. It isn't going to notice if we make five less blankets or twenty less chairs. You know who will?"

"Oh, please. Those idiots? You talk about them like they're a curse against society."

"They feed us. We give them goods to give to the Army and they give us a fair return. It's what the U.A. mandated, so it's how we have to operate. If people are too hungry to work... It's a vicious cycle," she walks in circles around the room. "By the way, Sanguine, we have almost half the Council on our side now, so cut the crap about 'showing the Council.'"

She paces the room, continuing to scan the note. "Ten recruits, though? That's good. You did better than me this month. Quinn's really making her way around to prospect," she frowns.

"Whatever," he says, "You've got Mac helping you, anyway."

"Mac hates me," Zurie laughs, "But she does help a lot. She doesn't care who she talks to. She'll probably be the reason we get caught."

Sanguine's stomach rumbles from across the room. The last meal he ate was small; two slices of jaw-breaking bread and half of an orange pepper.

Zurie sighs. She takes a sprig of mint from her pocket and hands it to him.

"I take them from Luna Bay. They quell the hunger a bit," she sighs again and turns her back to him, "Don't tell anyone."

"Thanks," he hesitates. "Look, there's a pretty clear solution here, even if you don't want to see it."

"We're not taking out the Council."

"Not the entire Council! Just a few of them. Whoever stands in our way," he pleads.

"Like who?" she asks, hand on one hip.

"Sam, for one. Makes sense to start at the top before anyone expects an attack. We get him out of the way and someone else takes his place. Maybe you, maybe MacRose, even."

"You really must think I don't pay attention. No one else supports that and neither will I. You'd rather die than see either of us lead everyone, anyway."

A noise outside the room silences them. He cracks open the door and checks the hallway. "I swear to God this place is haunted," he shakes his head.

"Probably," she says, thinking of all the needless death that's occurred over the years. "I support overthrowing him, but that's as far as I'll go. No more violence. I mean it," she shakes the paper.

"Who says I have to report to you?" he grunts.

"Majority rule, I guess," she smirks. She folds his report back up.

"Won't be a majority rule for long. You better be burning those," he mumbles.

She smiles at him and turns away. Her steps echo as she climbs a few steel stairs, opens the lid to one of the machines, and drops the paper in. "Oops," her face lights up.

"That could clog the filter!" he lunges.

"That'll really show the Council!" she shrugs and makes her way to the door, leaving him in awe behind her.

"Wait, Zurie," he stops her. "I need to talk to you about something else." She nods her head at him to continue. "I'm scheduled for the Test in six months. Sam told me yesterday."

3 / EDWIN

*7*oday the work is new to all of us. Instead of small crafts, they task us with creating handmade shelves. Although historically we've exclusively made toys, the shop has progressively grown to include all carpentry work. Not only must we assemble the shelves, but we must also decorate them. Fortunately, in a rare event, the powers that be have given us the freedom to choose our designs. The world so seldom allows creativity to blossom. I've learned to appreciate every moment of imagination I get.

Airlee's focus this morning is unbelievable. I glance up to watch her every few moments and admire the tranquility she seems to possess while working. As for myself, I feel clumsy and aloof using my hands to build something. However, mimicking her actions does me well; the guard compliments me on my mechanical abilities.

"Do now, think later," he laughs, "The trick to doing anything well is not to think too much. You may have never worked with wood like this before, but damn, you're good!"

His comments don't make me feel as bright as they probably should; I've already decided I don't like this poor excuse for a man. He doesn't have the skills a great leader does. If he's noticed me gawking at Airlee, secretly communicating through little notes and gestures, he hasn't made mention of it. He's spent his entire time with us getting an eyeful of various women. For all he knows, we're all conspiring against him as he takes in the views.

As he passes by me to review everyone else's work, I sneak another glance up at Airlee. She hides fear in her face with a false furrow in her eyebrows, the stoniness of her features giving away her phony attempt at apathy. Her hands shake – almost imperceptibly, but not quite – as she slows her work, choking with the anxiety of being observed.

"This one doesn't have a clue how to work with wood, does she?" the guard pauses behind her, openly glaring. Her face reddens under his gaze – his body is so close she can probably feel the heat radiating off of it. He takes in a long breath through his nose.

"When was the last time you showered?" he sneers.

Oh no. Some of the guards select a person to make an example of every now and then, regardless of wrongdoing. She keeps her eyes low.

"Do you like working with wood? I'm not seeing you act like it," he whispers loudly and grabs a lock of her ponytail. "Oilier than a catfish, as my grandfather used to say."

The rims of her eyes swell, fighting to hold back tears. It's true she smells bad, but we all do. I shake my head slightly and hope she sees. *Don't lose it.*

"Hurry up!" the guard slams his fist down on the table. Brushes fly up and roll off the workbench.

"Pick those up first," he turns away to audit the other side of the room.

As soon as his back is turned, the cedar drops from her spiritless hands like a dove shot from the sky.

She bends down to pick up the brushes and stays unseen for a while, pretending to search beneath the workbench for a lost brush. Her every little sniffle pokes at my heart.

* * *

Clean-up for the day consists of a little more than usual, but the guard doesn't keep us too late. Aside from the morning's comments, the day has been relatively uneventful and everyone appears to be thankful for it. A pair of workers high-fives each other on their way out. The guard grumbles.

We're not supposed to communicate closely with each other. The job is our calling and friendship can only distract us from what really matters. Cooperation is expected, beneficial;

friendship is not. Anyway, another day without serious incident. These days, it's good to say that.

Still, a bald man waits until the guard is watching everyone take off and gives Airlee the middle finger. The guard sees, but doesn't do anything. Neither does Airlee. She waits until the throngs of people in the hallway can give her enough cover to kick him behind the knee, sending him surging forward and onto other people. She blends in with passerby. Even I'm not sure it was really her.

Of all the people in the compound, there is no one the average worker hates more than those who give fellow workers grief. Some of us actually work to prove our loyalty. It's an unspoken rule among us that retaliation against such types is not to be reported. For the most part, the Council catches bad people, but someone has to police individuals like the bald man. They pretend to believe in the mission, but they're not really on anyone's team but their own.

Rather than scurry to my room to read my book, I spend a little time in the library. It's impossible to survive as a claustrophobe here, and the wider spaces the library provides make me feel more important – worldlier – than I really am. All this space, all to myself. The Most Privileged must feel this way all the time.

I meander over to the skills section and search around for

The Carpenter's Guide to Working with Wood. I'm curious about what Airlee's been learning that makes her so much better at handling the trade. If I excel quickly, perhaps I stand a chance at another promotion. If not, at least I might impress her.

The Council discourages friendship, but I can't stop thinking about her. I don't want to jeopardize my future, so I won't get too close – but she's something special. I can't quite put my finger on it.

I find the book quickly and leaf through its thin pages. In good condition, it clearly hasn't acquired much attention. The book includes mostly vague pictures with instructions: "Don't paint when it's humid;" "Wash all surfaces before coating;" "Don't glob paint onto your roller." I flip to the index to search for something more interesting.

I end up on the last page and notice blue ink at the bottom of the sheet. The handwriting is familiar, the same swirling ocean of letters Airlee writes. At first glance the scrawls look like notes, so I almost overlook them – but one word sticks out like a broken femur:

ESCAPE

4 / EDWIN

The word rocks through my skull and feels like it penetrates through the library walls, screaming out to the entire compound. *Escape.*

Why would anyone want to escape? This is home. Outside, we wouldn't even be able to feed ourselves. The War wages on, its poisonous remains destroying the environment. We provide and we are provided for, our safety assured. For that, we should be thankful.

I picture her eyes as though she's standing directly in front of me; the despair I saw in them earlier this afternoon comes back. The way the guard insulted her seemed personal. Maybe they're on to her.

A few bad apples don't mean the whole tree is dying. Just because a seemingly kind person is part of something so dangerous doesn't mean that I should be wary of every person I meet. I hope.

Locations throughout the building are scattered all over the page. Every one has Xs to their right, but the cellar.

ANYWHERE ELSE?

I try to imagine her saying the words on the page out loud. Would her voice be high pitched or low? Mousy or boisterous? Raspy or smooth? It makes me sad to know that neither of us will probably ever find out.

Footsteps approach. I shove the book back in its wide space and rip out some half-shredded publication about plumbing. This probably isn't the trade I want to get caught reading about, given that it's the only profession I could never stomach, but it is what it is.

I look up, pretending to check out the books on the wall diagonal to me. There she stands, an eyebrow raised, the slightest hint of anxiety in her eyes. She steps around to my side of the bookcase.

She nods at the plumbing magazine. I'm only opened up to its Table of Contents, so I hide its pages from her in a hurry. I hold up the magazine and nod veraciously. I'll never be interested in plumbing, but she doesn't need to know that.

She peers down and stiffens to attention. She nods gently once.

The carpentry book is sticking out just one or two inches, but enough to notice that someone else had been in her book.

An exasperated breath escapes her nostrils as her dainty hand reaches for the book. She stares at the cover as it rests on her palms. A sad smile forms wrinkles around her eyes. I can tell she's already accepting the facts.

She draws something black up out of her pocket – a pencil, obviously pilfered from the shop. She flips to a random page and scratches something onto it. She turns the book around and shows me.

Do you ever feel like we're treated like animals? it reads.

I gawk at the page for a moment, and then at her.

She raises her eyebrows again and exhales deeply. She's annoyed with me. Blood rushes to my face as my confusion mounts. Of all people, I truly don't want to believe that she's capable of a crime like treason. She turns the book back to herself and settles on writing some more. This time, she shoves the book into my hands.

Do you know what your fate is here? It's not pretty. She's underlined "pretty" twice. *They'll work us until they have no use for us, like cattle. Then they'll kill us.*

I've heard somewhere that all beautiful women find a way to make good men blow their tops; I suppose that in Airlee's case, her flaw is her selfishness. As an endangered species, we're lucky to even be alive. I take to the paper with a fury.

Yes, they might. Eventually we will be a drain on the system. I write.

Her eyes slice me apart. She turns the page loudly in search of more space. She scribbles quickly and her arm shakes as she passes me the book. Her handwriting is nearly illegible:

If you so much as question them, you're done for. They killed Alise and Murphy, my mentors. They were like parents. All for suggesting that we get better quarters.

Blotchy patches of red surround her eyes as they swim with fresh tears. The vision startles me momentarily. Hardly anyone makes an effort to communicate despair here. It's pretty much a given that we're all a little down at times, but getting seriously emotional can be deadly, what with our limited breathing making things difficult. It's been a long time since I've seen anyone cry.

Our sacrifices benefit others. I shake my head in agitation as I pass the book back. The Most Privileged show us the way every day. How does she still not understand what our community is about?

But why them and not us? she counters.

Visual alarms in the room flash red and white twice. "Fifteen minutes left before curfew," an automated woman's voice announces. In ten, the Nightly Report will begin.

Airlee shoves the book back on the shelf, her fingers lingering on its spine as she ensures it's all the way in. We lock eyes; in hers, there's a great sadness to behold and a long story to tell, if only she had better means to tell it. I wonder what she sees in mine.

Her eyes drift back to the shelf for a second. Suddenly her hand clasps mine, squeezing my work-hardened palm. Her face pleads with me not to tell anyone.

I take a moment. The silence in the library makes my ears ring.

Why not keep this little secret, at least the majority of it? She's allowed to have opinions and dreams, so long as she never acts on them and no one else finds out. But this will be the only time.

I nod my silvery head at her.

She grips my palm once more in a thank you and heads animatedly toward the door. I watch her as she goes and stare off at the doorway after she leaves, pondering. There must be a way to let the authorities know the Rebellion is using the library without clueing them in to her identity.

I reflect a great deal before lights out, letting my new book sit in its lonely spot on my sunken mattress.

The Least Privileged cannot survive in the outside world,

nor can anyone else, although we can trick ourselves into thinking the Most Privileged are immune. Most of us in the compound rely on nursing care just for nourishment; do these Rebels honestly believe that either dying slowly of poison or starving to death outside is better than life here? There's a reason we're stuck inside these walls. The brave soldiers fighting to win this war and strip the poison from our toxic wasteland have quite the jobs given that the people they're fighting for constantly do and desire things that could kill themselves. Unbelievable.

Even people on the outside of this facility work; nobody is exempt from the struggles of the world. There's so much to do that there aren't enough hands to do it all. Who would be stupid enough to put themselves and their people at risk?

Why does this suddenly matter to workers?

The intercom clicks on early. Sam clears his throat before speaking.

"Good evening, everyone. I hope you all had a fine day," he says. I know what to expect from here; he's going to announce which shops haven't met their productivity goals.

"The glass and metal shops underperformed quite significantly today due to another attack from the Rebellion. You are all encouraged to report anything unusual you may see to a guard."

How? Most of them have forgotten the sign language of the Least Privileged.

"Tomorrow is another day, my friends. May it be a better one." The intercom clicks off.

I wonder if he knows that tomorrow morning workers in those shops will be targeted for violence in the hallways, regardless of their involvement.

* * *

"Let's get this shit wagon on the road," a guard groans outside my room early in the morning. Occasionally, they accompany nurses during feedings to ensure that nothing goes wrong. It's usually a pretty awkward experience.

His footsteps echo as he follows someone down the hall.

My door clicks open without any warning.

"Exit the room," a man's voice booms.

I do as asked, struggling with some minor dizziness as I sit myself up. The room spins more as the guard grabs my arm and yanks me to my feet.

I wish I could have some coffee, I think briefly. Coffee hasn't been around for several decades. The virus wiped certain plants and creatures right off the map. Older generations could boost themselves up on something when they got tired at work; we have nothing, unless the back of someone's hand counts as encouragement.

"Edwin," the usual nurse comes into view as I'm forced against the wall. She turns to face the other side of the hall where others are pinned. A couple of reckless people sit with their eyes closed, napping. A woman across from me brushes through her bed hair with her fingers; she shakes her head at all the strands she pulls out and brushes them onto the floor. How thin we all are.

"My name is River Stone," she addresses everyone in a sweet – yet firm – voice. "My job here, as you all know, is to ensure that you are all well fed. We've had some issues with the Rebellion, so we're being audited today. We're assured that any backlash or refusal to be fed will be," she pauses for the smallest fraction of a second, "strictly punished."

A lone guard steps up.

"Behave yourselves and we won't have any problems. Am I clear?" His cold, gravelly voice runs shivers down my back.

I watch as River and her team sweep around the room, quickly setting up IV drips that will provide us with all the nutrients we need for the morning. One by one, the workers' bodies tense. Her focus never slips, expression never changes.

Down the hall Airlee sits, her lethargic head hanging. Her dark hair dangles restlessly across her face, knotted in multiple places. I didn't know that she slept in the same quadrant.

River approaches her after setting up her equipment. Airlee sits upright, back perfectly straight against the wall. Her eyes catch River's directly. She looks at her left arm and then back up to River. I can see the bruises from the end of the hallway. River mutters something or other to calm her down and instructs her to remove her sock. Airlee flinches as the needle pierces the skin of her foot.

River walks around the room and sets everyone else up. Finally, she reaches me. I hate being fed in public; there's something personal and vulnerable about it that makes the entire process uncomfortable. For a group of people that doesn't communicate much, a lot embarrasses us. Showing your disfigurements, for example, is looked upon the same way as whipping out your genitals.

One side of my mask droops, its loop having crested the tip of my ear, but perspiration glues it to my cartilage for the moment. I reach up to adjust it.

"You don't move a goddamn muscle," the guard barks at me. He shoves a black nightstick in front of my pale face.

The eyes of the woman across from me grow wide as she sees what's going on with my mask. The guard's back is turned to her. She flicks the back of her ear in a panic, looking all around the room. Everyone spreads the message while I sit helpless. River looks around, confused. A couple of workers look like they're laughing, but most of them gawk at me wide-eyed in horror.

"Edwin, your turn," River steps in front of me and sets up a new drip. I want to nod my head, but I stay as still as possible, chin down.

"I'm sorry I don't have any scents for you," she whispers, "with the new policies, good things are being taken away from everyone."

The needle's prick feels much sharper than usual; I'm so used to getting jabbed that I usually don't notice it, but in my anxiety, I'm hyper-aware of everything. I look her directly in the eyes in hopes of communicating the situation with my mask. She doesn't look up at me, so I seize the moment to study her face.

Bags sink her eyelids like anchors and her skin is papery and translucent. A few days ago, she could have fooled me for a teenager. I wonder for a second how old she really is.

She removes the tourniquet from my sticky arm and then goes back to her medical tools. She quickly returns to the IV and fiddles around with it, adjusting the drip.

Her moving arms create a tiny breeze. Like a scene from a bad dream, the mask pops off my ear.

She surges back, her saucer eyes glued to the mangled skin underneath the thin cloth covering. I scrunch my eyebrows together, trying not to imagine how she sees me, but knowing the reality all too well. The other workers sit up, still gawking at the spectacle as if they've never seen their own reflections before.

I fight back tears. The guard shifts in River's direction as she leans toward me, arm extended. She places her fingertips on my shoulder as the surprise evaporates from her eyes, pity replacing it instead. Her hand sinks heavier. I feel her tremble as she squeezes me – one of the many ways we workers convey an apology. Still, the mask hangs from one ear.

My own reflection hovers over me in her glossy brown eyes. The mangled, tumorous area where a mouth should be presents itself as a horrible wonder. The other workers look disgusted. Airlee probably witnessed the entire thing. I shove myself fully back against the wall, minimizing myself so fewer eyes can see. I don't dare loop the mask back over my ear for fear of being hit.

But River persists, inspecting me. I lower my head in an effort to hide, but she grabs my chin in one unexpectedly strong palm and tilts my head up.

"Miss, they're all like this," the guard says to her, "degenerates."

"I'm so sorry," she whispers. With a rapid flick of her wrist, she secures the mask's ear loop.

Her lips purse together and she turns way. She creeps over

to the first worker she stuck an IV in, glancing at me the whole way. One by one, she removes their IVs. When she returns to me, she pulls the needle out smoothly and wordlessly.

* * *

No one will even make eye contact with me in the shop. It's as though I've been cursed.

We've all heard the stories of someone's privacy being invaded – a worker's bunk being raided, a forced shower, someone's mask getting so worn out that it's practically translucent. I never expected myself to be a victim. A sliver of me hopes that the silence is just a friendly gesture to give me space. Somehow, I doubt it.

While I'm carving some intricate details into the face of a wooden train, Meyer calls me over. The king has unexpectedly reseated himself on his throne.

"I wanted to say thank you again for what you did," he utters, shaking his head. "I can't believe what we've come down to. No one wants to provide anymore, not for what they're given. It's a real sad state of affairs. If only we had more people like you, Edward."

I stare at him and settle on nodding, disregarding the fact that he got my name wrong.

"I heard about what happened with River this morning," he pauses, letting that sink in. The rumors must have spread like flu.

The racket of hammers and carving tools blocks most of the room from overhearing our conversation. "I want to offer you something. A story," he scratches his head as if doubting whether or not he should continue. "Once I was a man your age, just like you. I couldn't speak. I didn't know what juice tasted like, for God's sake," he laughs, forgetting that I don't have an opinion on it myself to even know how to react. He comes back down to Earth as soon as the dead air kicks in.

"What I mean here is, good things happen to loyal men. You saved my life in that shop and we both know you could have killed out of embarrassment today. And you didn't get those nifty little smellers they're supposed to put on your nose, did you?"

I nod.

"No one is, never again. And that memory, it never goes away. The want never ends. It's happened to me. However, lucky for you, the Council has decided that you haven't been rewarded properly for your services. They want to give you the one thing you probably really would kill for. But you have to help us with something first."

I make my left hand into a question mark.

He clears his throat, but his voice still sounds rough. "We got word from one of our contacts that the Rebels are using common areas to recruit people. We've noticed you going to the library. Could something be going on there?"

I crack open like an egg. I tell him everything he might want to know – about the library, the book – and exclude only a name. But it doesn't matter. If they had eyes on me, they have them on everyone. By the end of the conversation, I realize what I've done.

And what I'm going to get in return.

5 / SAMUEL

"Samuel," Alder whispers sternly in his ear, "it is time to wake up."

He blinks his eyes open and rolls over in a stretch. After lying for a couple of seconds, he settles back into his dream.

"Samuel," Alder rips the blankets up off of him, "I said for you to get up!"

He yawns and flips over groggily.

"Now!" Alder bashes his fist against a nightstand. "Roclear wants to see you."

This gets Samuel's attention.

* * *

"They're bringing in someone from medical this week. Hasek," Alder reminds him as he watches him rush to get ready. Clothes fly around the room in a frenzy as Sam struggles to find an appropriate shirt.

"The Council chose someone to cross over last night. We

figured we'd go on without you since you've been so very tired recently. We chose from ten names, all people who've offered some information about the Rebellion. We picked someone named Edwin. Based on his profile, he's a good, smart young man. Believes in us," he frowns.

"I'm glad I have you as my proxy," Sam says in a rush. He holds a long-sleeved purple button-up against his body while he looks in the mirror. The light in the bedroom isn't great, but he knows the shirt is at least free of holes. Maybe its regal color will be lucky.

"Don't make any mention of the Rebellion," Alder chides, "they will have a field day. As far as they are concerned, we picked a random name of the ten out of a hat."

"Will Roclear take this shirt the wrong way? Do you think the color sends the wrong message?"

"Samuel," Alder begins, "Forgive me, but I think your *face* sends the wrong message."

Sam goes silent for a moment. He then turns his back, removes his T-shirt, and puts the purple button-up on. It hangs loosely around his waist; he will have to tuck it in well in order for it to look right.

"There's nothing you can do to put more meat on your bones. It's time to get going."

* * *

"Mr. Hasek, thank you for your visit," Sam shakes his guest's hand and tries his best to smile. He watches as the thin man hands his yellow hazard suit to Alder, who hangs it up on a rack by the wall.

"Do not thank me, Mr. Garley," Hasek insists. His voice is dry and monotone. "I'd like to set up in the operating room now. The schedule this time around looks busier than usual," he eyes a small wooden crate on the ground.

"Those?" Samuel asks.

Hasek pauses awkwardly. "For the children. I'll be visiting tomorrow to check up on their health. Please save these for them and set up a room for me to sleep in."

Wordlessly, he collects his bulging medical bag and heads off to the lab. As soon as he's out of sight, Samuel picks up the box and peeks through the cracks. Alder has a fair idea of what's in it, but Sam isn't used to these kindnesses just yet. Medics have a history of feeling bad for the Least Privileged; they see the absolute worst of what humans can do to one another. The gesture isn't grand, or even helpful in the larger scheme of things, but brief moments of pleasure make their misery just a little more endurable.

"What's in the box?" Alder asks, playing dumb.

"They're mini chocolate, cream-filled cakes. Enough to last for weeks."

Alder frowns. "You know you can't give them those. It would be torture to never experience something as good again."

"I know," Sam pauses, "I'll give them to Quinn to sell. Maybe she'll have something for me."

Alder collects the hazard suit from the wall. "Are you ready?"

"As ready as I'm going to be for this asshole."

"Then put this on and off you go," Alder hands him the suit, "I'm going to go make sure the hall is clear."

"Don't you go sneaking desserts, now," Samuel laughs, though he doesn't much feel like it.

Alder's face lights up in a warm, fatherly smile. "It doesn't count as dessert if I eat one for breakfast, does it? Go on. You'll be fine."

* * *

The woody path to Roclear's camp is marked by a large, carved triangle on every sixth or seventh tree. Sam has only walked down it a handful of times in his life, but he's glad for that; the experience of warm sun, green foliage, and dirt under his feet don't relieve the cold dread he feels deep in his bones at the idea of visiting with the General.

It doesn't take long to reach the camp, but Samuel's breathing has grown labored inside the bodysuit. He takes a break for a moment to absorb his environment; after all, it could be quite some time until he's outside again. A tall iron wall surrounds the camp's perimeter, protecting it from curious onlookers – not that there would be many here. From as far as Samuel can tell, the camp is in the middle of nowhere, totally obscured by trees. Surely, however, someone is hidden in the woods, watching his every move.

He raps hard on the door three times and waits for an answer while he sweats in the hazard suit. Waxy, green leaves rain down from above him. Trees. They look so monstrous. Even if he could live outside the compound, he doesn't think he'd ever get used to them.

"Who calls?" a soldier shouts over the wall.

"Samuel Garley."

"You may enter," the soldier replies. He hits a switch and a section of the wall slowly folds down into a ramp. The machine creates vibrations in Sam's teeth.

He always forgets – maybe represses – what the soldiers look like. Even now, they're heavily armed. The man standing in front of him is shielded head to toe, automatic weapon slung across his chest and a grenade belt partially visible. Sam can't imagine why they pack that kind of heat out here.

Rabid squirrels, maybe. He stops himself from smirking.

"Let's go," the soldier gently shoves Sam forward. He follows behind him through a small courtyard and into an old brick building. The soldier abandons him at the door, letting another take his place. He leads Sam up an old set of wooden stairs, each step creaking violently.

He grabs onto the railing as a wave of nausea and dizziness rolls over him. The soldier looks back impatiently and opens a door. Samuel sighs and enters Roclear's office. After all this time, with all his resources, the man still hasn't replaced his grimy red carpet.

"Mr. Garley. Welcome. Please, have a seat," Roclear turns his head to a maid who has followed Sam in. He removes a glass of water from her silver serving tray, never offering his guest one.

"Take that suit off. You don't need it here," Roclear orders. He gestures for Sam to remove it.

He strips the suit off his body, acutely aware that Roclear is watching his every move. He tosses the hazard suit to the side of his chair.

"Humid day today, isn't?" Roclear says.

Samuel's tongue sticks to the roof of his mouth with thirst. He shakes his head. "I don't know what you mean, Sir."

"Ah," Roclear says, "I mean that it seems like it's going to rain out. Wouldn't you agree?"

"I couldn't tell you, Sir."

A dry silence licks at the air. Sam looks around the room while he waits for the General to speak. He notices an old, cracked fireplace with a macabre painting of a man holding a gun sitting on the wall above it. What he'd give to take the picture, frame and all, and light it up right in front of him.

"The time is approaching for your next volunteer to test the atmosphere," Roclear takes a deep breath, "Have you picked someone?"

"Yes, we've picked someone for the Test," Samuel answers, "a guard."

"Your guards are always willing to take one for the team. It amazes me. Really," he pauses, his smile rapidly fading, "Is he with the Rebellion?"

Shit. How does he know?

Sam fumbles for an answer. The correct answer.

"Don't lie to me, Samuel. I want an update on what the Hell is going on down there. I didn't call you out here so you could get some air."

Sam sighs loudly and meets the General's eyes.

"I suspect the man I've chosen is a part of some rebellion. It's a convenient way to push him aside. I'd like to jail him, but he's too dangerous to keep around," he takes a moment to compose himself. "General, no disrespect, but I need you to know what the problem is. Our workers are good people, but they're not machines. They can't work to the capacity expected of them."

"Have you tried *beating* some sense into them? Harassing them until they've no self-esteem left?"

"I'm ashamed to say yes. Sir, I am telling you what the problem is. Why won't you list– "

"Whine, whine, whine. That's why. I can't respect a whiner. If you had any leadership skills at all, you could make your people line up behind you and do as you ask, not because they want to do it for you, but because they want to do it for themselves."

"Good idea in theory, but if there's anything worse than misery, it's uncertainty. Please, Sir, my people are starving. They don't believe in us anymore when we say they're going to be fed."

"The food has gone to other compounds more deserving of it. We have some seeds and supplies you may collect on your way out, but that's all we will offer you," Roclear taps a pen mindlessly on his desk.

Sam feels the heat rise to his face. He tries his best to relax, bury the anger.

"Get up, Sam. Take a walk around the room," the General suggests, but Sam knows better. It's an order. He rises from his seat and walks to the other side of the room. His back is turned to Roclear as he continues speaking.

"There's more to this meeting than fixing that little issue. We've been keeping track of your births, as you know. These numbers have grown concernedly high. You now have more children hidden away than ever before. Can we go over this situation, please?"

"Our society functions under the knowledge that our genes have been mutated by chemicals. Most people are born disabled," Sam stares out of a window and watches two soldiers load up a truck. Indeed, in the short time he's been in this dingy office, black clouds have consumed the sky.

"And?"

Samuel shrugs. "Our workers no longer care about our policies surrounding children. It's become a strain on resources to discipline them all. We're also trying to make workers the most efficient they can be. To do that, we have to experiment. It hasn't been easy," he admits, "We only have a few people on the job."

What he doesn't say is that their doctor has been teaching them how to do it.

"It says here that you only approve who you call the 'Most Privileged' to have children naturally, is that right?"

"Correct," he looks down at his hands.

"Why?" Roclear smiles.

"The Council," Sam cringes, "believes that they're genetically superior."

"This is how you control the population. Preserving your best."

Sam's silence says it all.

"You have an interesting way of doing things, Garley. I'll give you that," Roclear shuffles his papers together, "but it's not enough. I'm quite shocked someone as soft as you can go through with experimenting on children, but that's your call to make. Others have been doing it for decades. The most it can do for you at this juncture is help you catch up to the rest of the groups out there. At any rate, it seems your issue is primarily with unapproved children. How you want to punish the parents is your call. In my shoes, I would vote for execution."

Samuel shuts his eyes. "The mother rarely survives. Having a child the Least Privileged aren't equipped for is suicide."

"But they do it, anyway," he nods.

"Yes," Sam says, "They do it, anyway."

"Whatever you decide to do, you're on thin ice. The compound is on probation officially starting now. If you aren't up to your quota within two to three months," Roclear passes him a sheet of paper, "many of your people will die and some will be moved to other locations."

He glances at the numbers on the page. "We'll never make

this!"

"Those numbers are *low*. And I have 'news' that will make your people very happy."

Sam watches him, confused.

"The government has suggested moving up the Test. The environment is not livable, but will be in a few short years. When that happens, the War will become *hot*. That ought to get them rolling," Roclear winks.

Sam doesn't know how to respond. If the plan doesn't work, horrible things will happen. If it does work...

Roclear will have the final say no matter what.

Sam nods and gets up to leave. He motions to pick up the suit.

"Oh, put that on later. Enjoy the rain. Be one of the first of your people to relish it. The smell of fresh rain is just wonderful."

Sam shoots him a dirty look and walks out of the office and down the stairs, dragging the suit behind him. It takes him a minute to notice the soldier tailing him.

"Let this guy through," he says to another soldier waiting at the wall. He directs himself to Sam, "You're lucky he's in a good mood today. He's shot men for less. Get moving."

The door's gears grind themselves open. Sam trudges down the ramp and back onto the path in the woods. The air smells of rotting citrus – the remnants of the old war chemicals, he guesses – and greenery. He slows down to enjoy the cool, whipping wind on his cheeks. Damn the toxic air.

An earthy smell emerges from nowhere, stopping Samuel in his tracks. Above him, something patters lightly against the leaves. Raindrops fall lightly against his forehead. He shuts his eyes for a moment, looking up at the sky. It's the first time in his life he's ever felt truly free.

If he could escape right now, how long would he last? A day? Two weeks, maybe?

A gunshot rings from somewhere in the woods, making Sam's eyes pop open. He doesn't know if the shot was directed at him, but he gets himself moving, anyway. The rain beats down on him all the way to the compound, soaking his clothes. He'll have to wash the mud off his shoes as soon as he can.

He knocks on the door and waits for Alder to answer it. It takes a few tries, but he grabs his attention soon enough. The door creaks open.

"Boy, you look like absolute *Hell*," he says, "Stay here while I get some fresh clothes for you." He begins to turn away.

"Alder, we're in really serious trouble," Sam pants. Alder faces him.

"I *know* we are. You can tell me all about it *after* I get you some clothes."

6 / EDWIN

*T*he operating table feels like ice, even as the intense fluttering in my heart pumps blood to my cheeks and arms. Voices float above as doctors in shabby yellow scrubs drift around the room, tools in their hands, their rich nonchalance welling a panic in me. None of their faces look familiar, but then again, I've never been invited to the other side of the compound before. They carry themselves with a strange confidence different from other medical staff. One of the men turns on an IV drip and steps away, never once explaining the process. What's the use in knowing if you don't have a choice but to obey?

I follow him around the room with my eyes for as long as I can. His thin paper facemask strikes me as a poorly timed joke. A new figure enters the room in identical scrubs, but I barely process him.

"Be at peace, Edwin," he says, leaning over me with concern. Before I know it, he whizzes out of the room. It takes me a moment to realize that the figure was Samuel Garley.

My eyelids droop and my vision blurs until my doctor is no more than a mere powder-blue blob. I feel like I can stay awake even if I let my eyes close for a minute, but before I know it, I'm no longer in the surgery room.

Thick blades of jade green grass cut into my bare feet. Again, I am outside. This time, though, I'm not alone.

I sneak forward, wincing with each step as the weeds stab me, and observe every detail of the land. Little water droplets have collected inside leaves and blanketed the lowest hanging ones with a thin layer of dark mud. I bask in the cool air as I drag my wet feet across the ground. The sun suddenly flares into my eyes from the thousands of beads of water, seeming to defy logical physics. A cloud lifts away as the golden light blinds me.

Only it's not the sun, not like I've ever seen it. This ball of light seems comical, almost alive in a sense, like something from an old cartoon book.

Likewise, the rest of my surroundings lean toward carica-ture. A monochromatic rabbit about half my size breezes by me, shouting "hello!"

I've never seen a real rabbit. This one is from *Charlie, the Carpenter*, one of my favorite books as a child.

Other chatty creatures emerge from nearby trees. An auburn fox greets me with "good day for a walk, isn't it?" before trotting across a sea of green and back into the dense forest. Birds chirp with absurd glee and a bear stumbles in my direction, nearly toppling over itself before coasting past me to something in the distance. I know it's a beehive without even looking. All of these animals I've only ever seen within the pages of stories.

The dream rapidly fades to grey as the real world bounces back. Hospital lights glare down at me from above my bed. If not for those, I wouldn't know if I was alive or dead; pain tears at every inch of my skull. I'm convinced it will blow apart if no one helps me soon.

There's no one in the room to reach out to. They've left me all alone. I grip the thin hospital bed until my fingernails feel like they might lift up. Rage bubbles inside me, the pain boiling over. The tension builds so much so that the inability to release it feels almost painful in itself. I lie grasping at the air, reeling, until I feel a vibration in my throat. The sound that comes from me is nothing less than animal.

I scream.

* * *

I wake on and off while a few nurses wheel me down a hall in a rickety hospital bed. The hall is ornately decorated, with paintings set over floral wallpaper, yet strangely dusty and dated. In the distance, past the ridges of my knees, the floor boasts bright red carpeting. They look soft enough to sleep on, but anything beats my worn out little cot.

Sleep. It's all I want, despite having just been knocked out. I shut my eyes. I've never seen a compartment as opulent as this, but the place could be studded with diamonds for all that I care; no matter where I look or what I focus on, I always return to the pain.

"This is one of our compartment wings. The others aren't as nice, but people mostly only sleep here. They used to be old offices, but they've been renovated over the years," one of the nurses says to me. I wonder how much of this experience I'll retain later.

A bump rouses me as we pass over a threshold into a deep room. Something about its furnishings boggle my mind, but I suppose it's because my body is full of drugs. Everything around me is red. Dark red carpets, light red walls.

"The sleepiness will wear off shortly," a nurse leans down and begins roughly undoing my new arm restraints. I only vaguely remember them even being put on. Another nurse works on ones down by my legs.

"This is where you'll be staying from now on. It's a lovely little studio all to yourself," the third nurse chatters to me while watching the other two. Even in my stupor I can tell that the chatter is part of a struggle to find something to do to fill the void left by the awkwardness of the situation.

"The view isn't much, that's for sure," one of them points at a blank, tar black wall, "but the space is nice. After all the restraint and bravery you've shown, we decided you would be better off away from the more wild ones, at least until things calm down."

"Maybe your stay in this compartment will be permanent. Hey, I'd like to live here more than in my own... At any rate, you won't want to go outside of this room for some time," one of the nurses giggles. "You look hideous right now. Sorry."

So much for friendliness. The room grows silent and stiff as a bone until finally they pick me up, one at each end and another guarding my middle, and place me on a smooth, red sofa. I notice in horror that my facemask has disappeared.

"It's worth it. We don't have the resources to enable everyone the way we did for you, but it's damn worth it. You earned it. Just don't look in a mirror for a while."

With that, the nurses administer some pain medicine through yet another IV and leave me.

The first thing I want to do is find a mirror, but I don't dare get up. The second thing I want to do is sleep.

My third wish, upon waking up, is to see Airlee. Somehow,

in my stupor, I've convinced myself she can take away the pain.

7 / SAMUEL

"Alder, get me my robes, please. There's a meeting today," Sam asks as he slips out of bed. Rather than sleeping, he read feverishly all night about anything he could get his hands on: history, the traits of a high-quality commander, botany, carpentry. Anything to make him forget about the rut he's been in.

In truth, he's been in a rut almost since the day he was born, but he won't make it if he looks at it that way, and so he carries on. He knows what few others know and he fights to keep alive. Happiness at this point means nothing. There is only survival.

Alder arrives at his bedside clutching a royal blue robe with a thick gold trim in his old, arthritic hands. Another robe is tucked into it, thin and silky and whiter than snow, but warm. Samuel's blood freezes as easily as a flimsy container of water left outside in the middle of winter. He does all he can to keep the chill out, even though he rarely succeeds. He doesn't like to be cold, and that's one thing his quarters will always be: cold enough to see his own breath.

"We have a great deal of work to do today," Alder says, his slim lips pursing into a solemn line. He's served Samuel for several years now, but never has Samuel known him without a face covered in the wrinkles of time itself. His white-grey hair becomes sparser every day, more and more noticeable as he refuses to cut it. One of a handful of elderly people in the compound, Alder knows everything Samuel does; he held his position once.

More than an advisor, he is also Sam's father and best – and only – friend.

When it came time for Alder to retire from his fifteen-year stint as the Head of the Council, it was no surprise to anyone that Alder chose his only son to succeed him; tradition made it common-practice. However, he was prepared to elect someone else if he felt his son did not deserve it. Fortunately, Sam was every bit deserving of the role – intelligent, caring, tactful, and skeptical in all the right ways. His son only needed guidance to use those traits successfully. Now, following tradition, Alder acts as an esteemed advisor.

Some would say he's more of a butler, but he ignores those comments.

Samuel faced some obstacles upon joining the Council, but he's found ways around thanks to Alder. His status has also played a role in his success; his father held the most important role, and his wife's parents were Most Privileged, born and raised, as was his mother. In fact, he and his wife are now among the few couples on the list for approval to start a family of their own. Alder started his late. Sam won't be an energetic parent, but still considers himself young.

Like anyone on the list of approved couples, he feels a lot of pressure to hurry up and have a baby. Alder has encouraged it, citing a child as a brilliant distraction from the chaos of the world. The thing is, he doesn't see the point in bringing a child into a disturbed world in the first place.

Alder watches Samuel as he shuffles about the room while getting ready for the day. Every so often he passes something to him – a shoe, a brush. With so many things to worry about pulling Sam in different directions, Alder tries to make his life easier in whatever way he can.

Whenever someone tells Alder about 45-hour workweeks before the War, he laughs. His entire existence is devoted to improving and maintaining the compound in order to ensure his country's freedom. This is his life. His calling.

At least, that's what he tells people, but he wouldn't trade his job for any other.

The two exit the ornate room, closing the door on the false warmth of red rugs and magenta blankets. The hallway feels like another world, industrial and metallic. It welcomes them with buzzing, cold teeth.

* * *

"We are here today to vote on the fate of one of our own, Edwin. He has shown himself worthy of driving up the ranks. Now we must decide on his job going forward," Samuel reads the top bullet point from a sheet. "With this as our first topic of discussion, I would like to begin by saying that I support making him a guard."

A woman with long, grassy blonde hair widens her eyes and stiffens up. She opens her mouth as if to say something and scans her eyes around the room, but she's so exasperated that the words do not come out.

"Agreed," one man says, scars marring a face that could have been handsome in earlier years.

"Glad we're on the same page, Meyer," Samuel nods, "MacRose, do you have something to say?"

The green-tinged blonde snaps her head in Samuel's direction. "Well, yes, I do have something to say," she begins, "the first thing being that you're all a bunch of idiots if you truly believe that he should be a guard. I'm not convinced he should even *be* Most Privileged."

"Oh, he wouldn't be with us here as part of the Council," Samuel counters, fully knowing the ridiculousness of his comment. She flinches.

"I understand that," MacRose explains slowly, her voice rising, "but what I don't understand is why *anyone* would put high hopes in him. He's *too* ambitious. He's going to burn out as soon as he realizes that being a guard isn't *enough* to create order here, and that he's still just a hamster on a wheel. If he's as smart as River says he is, you really think he's going to like what he sees? You know what he's going to do when he decides on his next ambitious move?" she pauses. "Those people are docile, like sheep. He'll do whatever we want him to, at least as it stands. Give him something menial. Make him believe in the work he'll do."

"We are all products of our own minds," Samuel says gently.

"Sure. But what happens when someone else does something good and there's no benefit for them in sight?" she looks around the room for help. A burly man with dark hair glances in her direction.

"Mac has a point. If people start to think of these transitions as special treatments instead of earnest, attainable rewards, it's going to ramp up the Rebellion. We can't feed them, but we can give one or two of them corrective surgery?

At last census, the working class made up eighty percent of our population. If the Guard can't handle them, everything we're fighting to restore will fall apart."

"This is why Edwin should be separated from the rest of the working class for a time," Alder throws in, sighing. "He is one of the few workers who expresses an interest in educating himself. The rest simply go through the motions. A man of his intellect can figure out how to escape the effects of his physical defects. It's best to pluck him out of that population before he gets pulled into the Rebellion."

The room seeps with silence.

"You're right. He may never self-actualize here, but he could easily change his mind about us over there. We should give him time to acclimate to this side of the fence. What do we tell the workers about his disappearing?" Meyer blurts, his scarred cheeks puffing out.

"If he becomes a guard, the Least Privileged will see him. It won't matter what we say. They don't buy the line about being promoted anymore, anyway," a woman with fiery hair says, concerned wrinkles conquering her forehead.

"That's probably because they know we're killing them," MacRose smiles sarcastically, "All things aside, they'd be able to communicate their problems to us if they had mouths to begin with. Take a look at the stats from this month alone.

Five guards have died and D Quadrant is in full anarchy. They aren't even working. We can't provide our end to the Barclays for trade? They don't feed us. They don't feed us? We don't work."

"*That's* why our underwear is sticking. Put anything in the laundry chute and you'll never see it again," Meyer laughs gruffly. River shoots a dirty look at him from across the room.

"We're a lot better off here than they are down the hill," Samuel lies. He stares at the wall across the room as he speaks, the old yellow wallpaper peeling and stained to a crusty light brown color.

"We don't know that, not really," MacRose says, "The Rebels took out external communications in G Quarter last month. Strapped a homemade bomb to a radio box. The only time we'll hear anything about other compounds now is after they've arrived for a bi-weekly inspection."

Samuel clears his throat and prepares to tell the room what he knows he should not. His oath to secrecy pales in importance to spreading the truth. However, as soon as he has their attention, he freezes. After all, they will ask questions they won't accept the answers to. They will panic. They've been lied to, and people have died in the face of those lies.

"I think we're prepared to move onto the next topic of discussion?" Alder suggests. "How about moving up the timeline for checking on the air outside? Maybe some good news will get everyone motivated."

The entire room relaxes, the tension evaporating.

"In a rare event, the Army has gotten in touch with us. The air may be free of chemicals within the next few years. We can go on *living,*" Alder's voice rises.

Gasps come from every part of the room. Looks are exchanged.

"How is this going to change anything?" the redhead asks.

"Mira, this means that we can bring ourselves outside to work. We don't need to stay cooped up. The Least Privileged feel like prisoners. This will be most exciting for them," Alder nods.

"If you call working up a sunburn 'fun,'" Meyer grumbles.

"I think it's fantastic," River pipes in, "We've all dreamt about going outside. Come on, everyone. This is exactly why we're working so hard. This is what we've been waiting for!" From across the room, Samuel scratches his neck awkwardly, knowing well what will come next.

"It's horrible," MacRose shakes her head, "It's absolutely horrible. I'm all for being able to spread our wings, but you're all forgetting something: we're still at war. If things are clearing here, they must be clearing elsewhere, too. Instead of worrying about poison, we have to worry about bombs and soldiers."

River frowns at her. At the core of most subjects, they agree, but Mac has a flair for the dramatic that River finds hard to tolerate.

"You may be right, but we need to take issues as they come. There's no point in fussing about possible doom and gloom in the future when we've got issues to work out today," Sam says, "Maybe we should start talking about that." He exchanges a look with Alder. They hadn't discussed revealing the news.

They spend the remainder of the meeting discussing motivational techniques, paperwork, and what life might be like on the outside. To their misfortune, they have completely neglected to address several issues, one being security in the greenhouse.

8 / RIVER

The air in the nurses' station reeks of sterility; alcohol permeates the room, drying out River's nostrils the moment she walks in.

She remembers a time when they used to do meaningful work. Now, all nurses do is feed the Least Privileged. That, and bandage up wounds created by animals with boots and batons.

Although her primary calling nowadays is to make sure that the unluckiest members of the community get fed, she has other responsibilities, too. On occasion, people catch colds that threaten to wipe out the entire compound. With vaccines and proper hygiene being the focal points of her sunniest dreams, she must tend to the ill with a mother's care. Soupmaking isn't her forte, but her sweetness is such that while treating others, her patients forget for a while that they're even ill. Rejuvenated and thankful just to feel normal again, people will say whatever is on their minds. Some call her nosy, or even a spy, but in truth, she's happy to be an ear. It's also the best form of entertainment she can get.

She knows for certain that the woman who lives in the small compartment next to hers is having an unplanned baby with her husband. The child will be born naturally – such children are unbelievably rare, the compound favoring complicated alternatives. With some luck, it will be among the first to leave the compound and settle in a safe, peaceful land.

If humanity is offered another miracle, the little one will go undetected.

The woman shared the information with River herself, but despite the display of trust, she couldn't bear to remind the woman where her child could end up. *We'll tell you she died. We'll say she's suffered a horrible defect – more horrible than usual – and that we killed her out of mercy.*

Sam will use the instance as an opportunity to reinforce the notion that only certain individuals should be allowed to have kids.

An unapproved child can never be Most Privileged. Never. In fact, depending on how the Council rules when someone finds out about the baby, the couple could get knocked down to Least Privileged status again. According to policy, they would be maimed as punishment. When the impure child gets a little older, she, too, will have her lips fused shut in order to reflect her status in the compound; the ability to speak would constitute as an advantage over everyone else. River has never understood the need for such barbarism.

Of course, some of the Most Privileged plead with the Council for forgiveness; they'll say goodbye to their children and never inquire about them again, promising to be loyal to the end of their days. It's convincing about fifty percent of the time.

The information River keeps goes way beyond the security clearance her position calls for; even the rest of the Council doesn't know some of the lurid facts that she does. Samuel protects everyone in the compound from uncomfortable truths, but for the most part, he can't resist her charms. For the past six years he hasn't, and she gladly accepts that he probably never will.

Samuel tows himself through the doorway, eyes fixating on the dusty, beat-up white monitor sitting on a desk across the room. Before the War, people entertained themselves on something called the Internet. Samuel can't imagine whole countries communicating over such distances, an entire world of knowledge stored inside an electronic box. He envisions little notes flying through invisible tubes in the air, but knows it can't have functioned this way. He's never used the monitor, but the antique serves as a reminder to keep striving for normalcy. Today, however, he just rolls his eyes.

"That's seven guards injured today alone," he mumbles. He throws his lightweight briefcase in a corner, the metal buckle pinging against the wall.

"Really? The air quality is getting worse. There isn't enough food to go around. People can't handle working long hours like this. Isn't there something you could do?" Silence.

"There's something going on with the vents either outside or in one of the rooms. I can't quite figure it out," River says.

"Animals?" he asks, hope filling his voice.

"Probably not," she answers.

"Could they be coming back around?"

She remains silent. Samuel knows how unlikely this is, but every six months or so he still asks for her opinion in the same way that a child would. Every time, she explains why she thinks the animals are gone for good.

Simply, humans smell bad to them. Whatever chemicals had been deployed changed something in human genes to make them smell diseased. In many cases, it's because people *are* sick, but not always so.

"Maybe," she smiles.

Truthfully, River doesn't know if the animals will come back; every now and then, a deer shows up on security cameras nibbling on Horsemint and sumac, its head darting up with fear at some mysterious sound before springing off into the tall grass. Other than that, no one reports creatures going near the compound.

While the United Army's enemies tried to prevent destroying the world with nuclear missiles, they missed the point. A simple, uncontained powder was all it took to ruin it all.

At a young age, River couldn't appreciate the grisliness of the War's beginnings. Now, she thinks about the ancestors she never met, wondering about what horrific things they had to endure in order to survive. She asks herself a lot of questions about the past. What if her relatives knew what a calamity the world would become? Would they have bothered at all? Would they have enjoyed their last warm showers and sweet indulgences before going dark along with the rest of humanity? To River, it seems miraculous that the country had managed to remobilize at all, given the losses.

"Sam," she reaches for his hand, "The only animals I'm sure of are inside this building."

He nods. She's right, but there's not much he can do about it.

* * *

The red floor of the bedroom creaks underneath her bare feet as she makes her way back from the bathroom. She tiptoes closer to the bed, lifts the blanket, and eases herself under the covers.

"Don't bother being quiet," Samuel's raspy voice mutters, "I could hear an ant crawl tonight."

She stares at his figure in the dark, her eyes still adjusting to the fresh darkness of the room.

"What's wrong?" she asks, struggling to wake up.

"I'm thinking of how different it used to be when we were younger," he answers. She watches him stare at the white emptiness of the ceiling as if he can see through it into some other dimension. Probably wishing he was there.

"God, I barely remember being a kid," she laughs, "Everything we do now just seems to take up so much space in my head."

"It absorbs a lot, doesn't it?" Samuel pauses. "I still remember happier times, although some days I wish I forgot them. We had new clothes and fresh fruits. The air smelled clean and no one worried about rebellion in this tin can. People were just happy to get food and a good place to sleep, you know? Alder had a way of keeping everyone in line that I don't have."

"Your dad had all it took to be a great leader. It didn't happen overnight, though. You're getting there," she resettles her position on the bed and faces him. "What about the Least

Privileged? We were *born* lucky, at least. They've *never* had what we've had."

"We used to have a sort of symbiosis. Not anymore. They think that the way we live is wrong. Maybe they're right," Sam sighs and clenches his fists involuntarily, "I don't know if they even need us as much as we need them. They get smarter every day, learn how to get past their flaws."

"Don't say that, Sam," she reaches over and places her hand on his chest. "We need them and they need us, whether people understand it or not. We have to do the things we do in order to survive. We just have to figure out how to do better."

The sound of his sigh fills the room. He cups his forehead in his hand and rubs his scalp.

He laughs. "None of it's fair. We do so much work for so little. Less and less every year."

"Have you tried negotiating with the Barclays?" she asks.

"Of course I have," he fibs, "and there is nothing they can do. If we don't start producing, we're going to starve. And I mean *really starve.*"

Leaning on her elbow, she looks down at him and rubs his chest in gentle circles, hoping to coax him into sleep during a lull in their conversation.

"Our communications with the Barclays ceased. I don't know what kind of technical issue we're looking at now, but we're dead-zoned. We're on our own until their med officer leaves and gives them the message. Couldn't we try to communicate with the Army ourselves? Why use a middleman for trade?"

"They're closer. They won't budge. Tried it."

The small, antique clock on their bureau ticks away as a silent moment passes. Finally, River speaks up again.

"How is Edwin doing? I haven't seen him since the operation."

His voice brightens, but he speaks slowly, half in the room and half asleep. "Shocked, but well," he says, "Hopefully he'll get the life he deserves. Loyalty like that should be preserved."

River ponders his answer for a moment. "Do you think he'll adjust to life here? It's so different than it is in the worker units."

"I think he'll do just fine. He'll be grateful."

"The riots are getting bad. You never truly know what anyone's thinking anymore. Any day, one of my girls could be taken hostage. Working for me is like moving in and out of a warzone," she pauses, "Edwin is *smart*. I worry he could have formed his own ideas. We have to watch out for radicalism."

He grunts. It's not the first time they've had this conversation.

"Why can't we tell people that we're not responsible for the way their lives are? We're under the gun, too. Everyone knows about the trade deal," she tapers off. Yes, everyone knows about their relationship with the Barclays, but no one truly cares; at the end of the day, certain workers will always see the Most Privileged as the reason they can't speak, eat, or work easy jobs. River puffs out the air she's been holding in her mouth as she realizes she's answered her own question.

Samuel doesn't respond. Quiet snores escape his mouth with each slow breath. She gazes at his peaceful face, recognizing with sadness that these moments of unconsciousness are the most relaxed she sees him.

Despite what Samuel's broadcasts claim, they are losing the War; River is convinced of it. She has never met any of the highest ranked officials from the Barclay compound, but what little she's heard about them has turned her off. They possess the ability to wipe their little clan right off the map. Even if they need their ceramics filled with nails and ridiculous alcohol flasks to trade with the United Army, the fact is that with one less compound in the picture, the Barclays have a shot at more food for themselves. Sam has always said that civil war was bound to start; most likely, it already had.

Based on the rumors she's heard, the Barclays can barely step out of their homes, where the curtains are drawn and the reek of the diseased grows. Their bodies can only handle so much physical activity, but the compound is huge; thousands of guards, the healthiest men in the little city, protect its boundaries. Other compounds rest under their thumb, as well.

How long can this last? River wonders.

Alone in the darkness now, she snuggles closer to Sam, letting his warmth soothe her chilly skin. She loves him, truly and purely. Their relationship began out of mutual interest in each other, although a fair number of people still whisper that she takes advantage of him, influencing his decisions too much. Despite what everyone else might think, she takes comfort in her intentions. Their relationship has never been hidden and she trusts that he's an honest man.

Still, she can't shake the feeling lately that he's keeping something secret.

He pulls her close with one arm in his sleep. She drapes hers around him, but lies stubbornly awake. The problem with being comforting is that often no one is left to comfort you.

* * *

It's around 6 o'clock in the morning when her eyes flutter open. Somehow, the sleeping hours have slipped away and doomed her to repeat the day before in a never-ending cycle. She takes care not to wake Samuel, even though he sleeps next to her as still as a fallen tree trunk, snores louder than the compound's worst exhaust pipes. She creeps out from under the blankets, throws on a shabby pair of green scrubs, and sneaks to the hallway.

Sometimes, walking down this dead metallic straightaway, she feels as though she's in a submarine from an old movie. It's an exciting thought, although she doesn't imagine in real life it would feel that way for long. Unable to escape, it would just wind up feeling like more of the same.

She turns the corner while flipping through her notes about Edwin's surgery. She has a few technical questions for the medical officer, small procedural things she'd like verified. She always wants to learn more, especially if it will help her keep her people healthy. She can only help so much until her skills become useless – she's lost track of how many people she's lost to appendicitis and tooth infections. Fortunately, he's open to helping, even if he's not exactly the most sociable man. Even though his people completely oppose it.

As she's reading, her chest bumps into a solid force, knocking her off balance. She clutches at the ugly, aged moldings on the wall for support. She quickly careens sideways and starts to lose it. She fights a look of aggravation before looking up.

Meyer peers down at her, distant, but aware he's knocked someone over. He simply stands there and watches her struggle to right herself.

Her grip manages to keep her upright well enough to avoid

landing on her rear end. She abruptly straightens up, her nose an inch away from his chin. She glares at him in defiance.

"You making sure I showered this morning, Riv?" he asks humorlessly. "You know I didn't. And neither did you."

With that, he sidesteps around her and wordlessly strides down the hall."

"What the Hell is wrong with you?" she mutters, but it's like speaking to thin air.

9 / ZURIE

"Zurie," a man mutters in passing. He nods his head to her and continues on his way.

She smiles to herself and looks around the hallway. There on the wall, someone has spray-painted her name in large letters alongside a set of three circles – an old symbol for the atomic nucleus. In the center where the circles meet, the artist has placed a cross. Further down the hall, another such symbol rests, a heart filling the center of this one. It's one of the easiest ways for her followers to safely communicate their needs. A smear of paint on any given segment of the circle tells her what quadrant the artist resides in, helping her eventually locate them.

The adults in Bourney absolutely love her. Someone in D Quadrant needs medical attention. That could prove a little difficult, considering the anarchy there. *Thank you, Sanguine,* she rolls her eyes.

She knows all she needs to do is bat her eyelashes at a guard to let her through, but she'll have to wait for the right duty schedule. Only a follower or a complete idiot would let her in.

A team has already begun scrubbing the graffiti from Bourney; a fruitless act. Another will be there by midday.

She raises her hand to the guard posted outside of the lab, her head held high.

"What's ya need?" the man asks, never rising from his seat.

"Classified," she winks.

"Just go in and get it. I didn't see ya," he looks back down at the book he's reading.

Zurie lets herself in.

"How many you taking today?" Dr. Hasek hurries out of a side room.

"Twelve, or however many you've got. We have a problem with the latest flu."

"I don't have any flu shots, but I can help you with the mumps," he says, "At least if they're going to have the flu, they won't have the mumps, as well." He reaches out to give her a basket full of needles. She grabs it gingerly.

"How do you get away with giving us this stuff?" she asks.

"When you're the one making it and taking stock of inventory, you can afford little kindnesses here and there."

She sees it in his eyes, but can't bring herself to point it out. He pities her and her people.

"Thank you, Dr. Hasek," she turns around to leave. "Before I go, how did the new guy make out on his surgery?"

He grimaces. "Don't expect a quick recovery. He lost a lot of blood. It's a good thing," he pauses, "that some of the children are O-Negative."

It takes her a second to comprehend what he's just said. He's gone behind her back to collect blood from the children. He's a good man, but that doesn't prevent her from wondering if this was the first time. She wants to hold her tongue.

He nods his head at her as if to dismiss her from the room. *Well, screw it.*

"Have you been doing this for a while?" she watches as he turns. "Donating the blood."

"I thought you knew," he shakes his head, "I only do it when I have to. Believe me, I'll be the last to take advantage of a child." He returns to his work.

She stares at the back of his head. Why does he care so much about the compound? It doesn't make sense.

"What's it like where you come from?" Zurie inquires.

"It's difficult to understand unless you've been there," he replies, readjusting his thick glasses, "Everything is whole and everything is falling apart at the same time. It's not a lot different than here. They don't allow us to have kids at all, though."

"Why's that?" she asks without thinking.

"I think you know the answer to that," Dr. Hasek's voice has grown cold.

"So... How do you keep expanding your population? You have to maintain it for the long-term somehow."

Dr. Hasek heaves a sigh. "I think it's time you be going."

Zurie's shoulders sink in disappointment. She'll take any information she can about how other compounds operate, but it's not always so simple. Some subjects, like children, are touchy. She knows she's pushed her limit this time. Her hip nudges the door open and soon she's out of his sight.

She grips the basket's wicker handle until it hurts her palm, then relaxes her hold, repeating the same motion over and over again. If anyone stops to ask her what's in the basket, she has no way of explaining. It's best to get to the kids before anyone asks any questions.

"Hey, what do you have there?" a voice calls from around a corner behind her. "A basket of candy for me?"

Zurie clamps her eyes shut for a moment. A splinter from the basket cuts into her hand.

"Either walk and talk or go away," she says.

He catches up to her in three long strides. "Are those for

the kids?"

"Yes," she whispers, "Can you please shut up?"

"At least you said please," he grunts. "Who's the new guy coming over?"

"His name is Edwin. He's going to be a guard. I want you to keep an eye on him. Don't let him get away, but don't you dare turn him into some brick-throwing liberal idiot."

"Ouch," he pauses. "How's he doing?"

"The MO says he's taking the change hard. I've no doubts he's heard a comment or two. Good news is, he can speak. Everything went the way it was supposed to."

"The comments alone can make you want to turn. You remember what Meyer said to me the first time he saw my face?"

Zurie looks blankly at him. It's been years.

"I believe the exact words were, 'put some lettuce and buns on it and you'd look delicious.'"

"I bet he was trying to make you laugh," she looks down.

"Yeah," he says, "but it fucking hurt. I laughed for my own good, but it hurt. A lot. Took three months for me to fully heal, and three months later a group jumped me."

"I'm sorry for that. They paid. I remember that much," she whispers.

"Quinn's not as open to helping us as she used to be," he looks to the side as he talks, "Greedy bitch says her price has gone up."

"She always does this," she whines, "Have you tried stealing?"

He nods. "Time for bigger prizes, I think."

She stops in front of the entrance to their hall. "Is there something else I can do for you, Sanguine?"

He stands there, emptily processing her change of attitude. He's exhausted. Between organizing a rebellion and actually working, he's had no time to be himself and his nerves are frying as a result. He opens his mouth to speak –

"Hello there," a familiar voice calls from behind Sanguine, "I didn't know you two were friends."

Zurie pops her head out from behind her accomplice, feeling guilty as she watches a confused look spread upon Sam's face. Her knuckles turn white against the basket's handle.

"We're not," Sanguine says without looking at him. "I have an infection I needed to ask a nurse about," he scowls, "Thank you."

Zurie offers Sanguine a brief smile and heads directly to the children's labor camps, dodging flurries of silly questions along her route. The quietude that overcomes her once she's inside Bourney's boundaries comes as a relief.

Enough dawdling around.

10 / RIVER

*W*hen River arrives at Edwin's door, she isn't sure what to do. Does she announce herself? Does she let herself right in? He was put under some pretty heavy sedation and she doesn't want to scare him. She opts for the least polite solution, fearing that if he hears her he'll just ignore her, anyway. Her keys jangle together as she locates the correct one and unlocks the door.

"Edwin?" she shouts as she peeks her head in the doorway.

A grunt emanates from the couch in the middle of the living room. She approaches it slowly from the side, flinching as she realizes that the noise of her voice made his head throb. As she rounds the corner of the couch, she takes note that its fabric is blood red. Whoever designed the compound certainly favored the grotesque color.

This compartment is bigger than mine, she observes.

"How are you feeling?" she feigns a smile.

Edwin taps his head while shaking it slowly to signal that he's in pain. He takes both hands and breaks an imaginary stick as if to say *I feel broken.* River's face scrunches with pity and a new wave of pain crashes over him. He cries out, the sound strangling itself in his throat.

River loads up a syringe with a dose of morphine and inserts the needle into his right arm. He jumps a little at the jab.

"It's only a bit of pain. You'll feel better in a while," River coaxes.

What she's really thinking is, *I don't know how this can possibly work at all. Your entire face has been reconstructed.*

"When you recover more, we'll get you in speech therapy. We'll teach you how to eat and do all the things you haven't been able to do. That will be nice, won't it?"

Edwin doesn't respond.

"I have to check your skin to make sure an infection hasn't set in. A bit of your scab might come off, but I'm not going to hurt you. It'll be over fast."

This is the moment she's been dreading. She hates it every time.

She watches him as she peels up the edge of the bandage. His eyes snap shut as he passes out, allowing her the freedom to investigate. The morphine will knock him out for a good part of the rest of the day.

Small bloody flaps cover the bottom portion of his face. She parts his new lips and looks inside his swollen mouth with a flashlight. In days to come, she'll have to force Edwin to wear gloves as his skin begins to heal and dry out, bringing on an irrepressible desire to itch. It's during this stage that her patients are most vulnerable to infection.

She sighs and applies medication where she can. If she's diligent and his body handles the recovery well, there won't be much scarring. Her nose burns as tears rise to her eyes. She swallows them down in dry gulps.

It will take months for this to heal, if Edwin manages to survive at all. Only a few have let go over the years. Hasek knows what he's doing. But it doesn't stop his patients from looking like monsters.

PART TWO

11 / EDWIN
1 Month Later

The black blades of the ceiling fan whir by slower and slower the longer I stare at them. There is a certain cleanliness to them that irks me. I've been here for what feels like months, but they've gathered no dust.

Today the Most Privileged will tell me about my new position and let me know if they think I've recovered well enough to start. After a month of therapy, I can speak; or rather, I try to. River understands me, but not so many others put in the effort. I'm confident that in time, I'll be capable of assimilating to my new home, working less manual labor. To tell you the truth, though, working with my hands is what I enjoy.

The most esteemed positions here – aside from being a member of the Council – are among the Guard. The thought of sitting around all day doing nothing but pushing buttons and barking orders unleashes a well of anxiety in me. I'm not ready for that yet.

I adjust my back on the couch. It's where I've spent the last month nearly going out of my mind, my behind permanently imprinted on the cushions. The nurses brought in books, sure, but there's only so much that one can read without their eyes becoming strained or the words blurring together into meaninglessness.

The most unfamiliar words haunt me at night. Verisimilitude. Superannuated. Effluvium.

I've attended speech classes with others like me. There are just a few of us. One has been going to classes for six months and another for a year. The one going for a year told me that he's been pulling the wool over the eyes of the Most Privileged since almost the beginning; he never wanted one of the "esteemed" jobs.

The Most Privileged have given me opportunities to socialize, grow, and earn some self-esteem. I'm afraid and beyond pleased at the same time. It seems wrong to take advantage of them.

My compartment completely lacks mirrors. It's no question why. It was the first thing I noticed once the grogginess and pain wore off, and I started wandering the place. Scarred, tumored, or as smooth and artificial as a doll, I was grateful I couldn't see myself. For two weeks I snuck glances at myself in reflective surfaces, but could never make myself look long enough to take in what I'd become. The surgery made a mess of my face. I just *knew* from the pain I was in.

When I stirred my new tongue around in my mouth, nothing made sense to me. The cavity was large, too large. I felt teeth, obviously implants, square and symmetrical. Now, my jaw gets sore all the time; River claims it's because of stress and that I must be grinding my teeth. I also kept biting my tongue at first, but I seem to be getting away from that now.

It's ironic that they gave me a mirror as a privilege over a month ago even though my reflection only made me sad. A part of me wonders if it was a deliberate choice, a tact to keep me moving forward.

I knew I wouldn't find the same person staring back at me in the mirror, but a week ago I decided I needed to take a look for myself.

"Muhhrah, pease," I requested during a feeding. I could have explained why I wanted one, bore my soul, but I think it must have been obvious.

Speaking, though not my least favorite thing in the world,

has grown to be pretty high on that list. People don't much care to communicate when the best I can do is with my hands.

"What?" River asked. Her eyebrows scrunched; she was trying her best.

"Urrar," I flinched hearing myself. She reached into her pocket and produced a pen and paper. I wrote down what I wanted.

She gave me a little smile. "I've got just what you need if you're sure you're ready."

I nodded despite her look of concern.

The next day, she brought me in a little hand mirror, its reflective surface flecked off with age in some spots. I suspect that she wasn't supposed to do this, but I don't know for sure.

"I do my makeup in it," she said quietly.

Makeup. She can get makeup, but workers can't get fed properly. I stared at the mirror in her hand, contemplating this for a few seconds.

They've stopped feeding me by a tube. No one announced it. It just happened one day. Around this time, my sense of smell reached the normal threshold – something I should be thankful for, but I'm not. My compartment may look sterile, but the reek is something terrible. I'm told the pungent aroma is a combination of mold and corroded metal, but I can't be sure. I have no memories to compare to. I mostly miss the days when I couldn't smell anything unless someone placed it directly below my nose.

The day they stopped feeding me by a tube, they brought in a tiny jar of what the nurses call "baby food." The orange mush they first spoon-fed me was labeled "Carrot." It expired years ago, but should still be safe to consume, they said. I wasn't a fan of the Carrot, but flavors since have impressed me. They fill a void in the pit of my stomach that I didn't even know existed. And it sounds strange, but the tastes made me happy.

Why should sustenance make me happy? We need air to breathe and that doesn't make us *happy*.

Despite everything, my heart expanded when River brought in the mirror. If I didn't look like an ogre, I thought, perhaps my self-esteem really did stand a chance. She gave me the opportunity to get used to myself.

"Go on, take it," she urged gently.

I hesitated. Did I really want to do it? What if looking into the mirror completely destroyed my confidence? I searched River's eyes for motivation, but I could tell that she wasn't going to encourage me much. She wanted me to make the decision on my own. I figured in a rush that it would be better to tackle the issue sooner rather than later, come to terms with my new self. At best, I looked like the much thinner version of someone out of an old-fashioned modeling magazine.

The mirror's handle felt cool in my hand, its face deliberately turned away from me. As I held it, River checked if her eyeliner was smudged, making me crack a little smile. I looked down and took a deep breath.

I flipped the mirror toward myself quickly, startling her a little. I kept my eyes on her so as to avoid myself. This woman was my anchor.

"You don't look bad, you know. You have a handsome face. Your scars need to fade more, but you'll be fine soon."

My reflection revealed a completely new person. My skin, once so white as to be nearly translucent, had taken on a tanner shade that – while not yet totally healthy – suited me. Dull tufts of black hair sprouted among the grey. I had color. For a moment, I wondered if my image was some kind of sick joke, another man's image for show. I touched a black splotch, watching my reflection mimic my every ginger move.

"It'll all grow back in your right color eventually," she said, relieved by my reaction. "It always does. You just have to keep healthy. Eat when you can," she continued, her words like afterthoughts.

I've seen my face very few times without a mask. As a means of survival, the ugly can find beauty in anything as long as they search hard enough. The heart cannot grow or even maintain itself while drowning in self-pity. I found beauty in my eyes, but I was no longer the semi-faceless man. Looking at myself that day, I didn't know which feature I liked best.

The pain was worth it, after all. The surgeons worked way beyond my expectations. I wouldn't fit in on the cover of a catalog, but if not for some medium-light scars around my mouth, I could fit into the world I actually lived in.

At least, I could physically fit in; I'd blow my own cover the second I spoke. I wondered what opportunities might emerge for me in the future. And if my speech would be a hindrance.

I opened up the lips I'd exercised for weeks and found a miraculously perfect set of teeth. White, square. A salesman's smile. To be honest, they were too perfect. Unnerving, actually. I suddenly found myself foreign and had to look away.

"What's wrong?" she asked, tilting her face to the side.

I shook my head.

"You can speak now. Come on. Give it your best try. You had to have learned something about speaking just by listening to people doing it," she coaxed.

I just looked at her, those big eyes sparkling. She had no idea what I was going through.

"You know," she said, "We'll want you back at work soon. Your strength is back. There's no real reason for you not to go. You can wear a mask until you're comfortable, of course, but everyone has to do their part. You won't even have to speak most of the time. Some of the Most Privileged can't."

I tilted my head.

"Most of the guards who wear facial coverings can't speak. Their operations didn't go as well as yours did," she frowns.

"We'll be moving you to a guard's position, but it's unofficial, so I didn't tell you that. Something low responsibility, in the background, at least until you're used to things here." She saw my eyebrows furrow. "I'm sorry," she added, "The Rebellion *has* gotten worse. It's not just a rumor. Our food stocks are low. People are attacking guards left and right. We need the help," she said half to herself.

"I really shouldn't have told you that," she exhaled, easing her body up off of the couch. Her hands trembled and her eyes darted around the room.

"Listen, Edwin. Do what they say, okay? They'll give you everything you've ever wanted in life if you just do one or two things for them, no matter how you really feel," she said. "And what I said about being a guard? That stays between you and me."

I watched her shuffle out of the room while my head spun. It didn't stop spinning for quite some time. Finally, I concluded that since I didn't have a choice in my occupation, I might as well stop considering the risks.

* * *

"Edwin, you may enter," Samuel's voice booms from behind the Council chamber's door. An expressionless guard standing next to the entryway gently nudges the door open, its hinges creaking away with every inch. My feet drag me forward at a snail's pace until I'm positioned in a large alcove next to a guard whose body smells like ginger and lavender; a wonderful combination in theory, but in practice so rich it makes me want to vomit. I only know these scents because of small items nurses have brought in to expose me to new things – perfumes, candles, old food.

The sturdy door closes behind me with a gentle thud. The many faces in the wide room study me, their eyes glued to my mouth, not bothering to disguise their opinions of the surgeon's work. One woman, a surly-looking redhead, nods in approval. Not one motions to introduce themselves. Even good 'ol Sam lets a moment pass. We officially met once before during a speech therapy session, but only as a courtesy.

I knew I should have just worn a mask, but that felt rude somehow. I never stopped to think of myself before leaving my compartment, and how I would feel in a situation like this. I only thought of how unappreciative I would seem if I didn't act the way they'd probably hoped I would.

"Edwin, as you know, we've called you here today to discuss your new role within the community. It has already been decided. In light of your transition, we will offer you what training we can," Samuel says, folding and unfolding his hands slowly. "We've decided to make you a guard. You will be the apprentice of Wayne Meyer," Sam says. He attempts to smile.

Red-hot hives blaze on my chest as my nerves reach high gear. It's only a matter of time before they lick their course all the way up my neck.

"Why dis position?" I ask, flinching at my poor enunciation.

"We believe you would be well suited for it," the woman with red hair says.

"Why not anudda position?"

"We need smart men like yourself as guards," Sam replies.

"No need fuh smart men in udda positions?" I say. My eyes bore into his skull.

"Are you saying that you don't want to be a guard, Edwin?" The woman with the red hair asks me. "It's the highest honor, aside from leadership. There is no room for lost potential here."

The threat is venomous, but all I can focus on is her scowl. That beautiful, wretched look. I will strive to model future scowls after hers.

"Now, now, we don't need to go on saying things like that,"

Sam says, "But why not give it a try?"

"People die," I say, trying to keep my words at a minimum in fear of screwing up.

"Yes, people do die every day in this world. Sometimes they're sick and sometimes they're killed. Our food supplies are running short and the problem grows deeper every day when the men in the greenhouse have to be relocated and sent to police the most violent areas. You'll be sent around, Edwin, I won't lie to you about that, but you'll do just fine. We hope you'll set an example for others. If you work hard and you do what's right, that will get you places."

My heart is ready to take off out of my chest. Beads of anxious sweat drip down my face. I nod my head.

"You will start tomorrow. Be awake and ready at 6 AM."

Say goodbye to sleeping in and getting an adequate recovery.

Sam's eyes shift to the door, hinting that it's time for me to leave. I turn halfway to the door and stop.

"Faces," I say, gesturing at my own mouth, "Why are dey different?"

A snicker casts its way across the room. The redhead perks up. She squares her shoulders.

"You were born that way. Your kind is genetically inferior. We fixed you."

Your kind.

* * *

My eyes flood open and let the light gush in. I feel a wave of terror, like I've been jolted by lightning, and I know immediately why. The clock only verifies my suspicion. It's 5:45. If I'm not ready in 15 minutes, Meyer's going to kill me.

I scramble off of the couch to the kitchen and open a jar of some kind of mashed red fruit. My fingers shake as I pry off the lid. I only scoop out a few mouthfuls of the sickeningly sweet pulp. *Tick, tock.*

I almost run out of my little compartment, but realize I've forgotten water. It's been a real challenge for me to remember to take some everywhere. I've been reacquainted with an IV several times due to dehydration.

I pour myself a large cup from a yellow gallon and notice a book sitting on the counter from the corner of my eye. I finish pouring and leave the gallon in the corner. There's a note attached to the book's cover:

Edwin,

I found this book when we cleaned out your cell. I forgot that I still had it. Perhaps you would like to continue reading it? Good luck at your new job.

River

Has she snuck in recently or have I just not noticed *The Short Mysteries of Drugsberry* resting on the kitchen counter? Regardless, the book floods me with odd memories. It's been four weeks since I last set foot in my room. My room, which River called a cell.

I wonder what Airlee will be doing today back in the shop. I thought of her during the hardest parts of my recovery, struggling to remember details about her the more time stretched on. What does she smell like? What color are her eyes? I remember a vagueness about her and worry that I've recreated her in my mind. If I see her again, will she be as I remember her?

A twinge of sadness washes over me as I realize Airlee and I will never work together again. At least, not in the same capacity.

I wonder if anything has come from my hint to Meyer.

Something had to be said – the Rebellion will destroy the compound if it's allowed to flourish. It was the right thing to do. Still, every time I think about her, a dark pit weighs down my stomach. I know the Council takes threats seriously – sometimes too seriously. If they caught her for so much as looking into the Rebellion, she won't survive, and that's my fault. Maybe I should have tried harder to dissuade her from joining before saying anything to Meyer.

I grip the book in my hands, thinking about the library we both love. I hope she's not spending much time in the trades' area these days.

The healing and therapy processes have devoured practically all of my free time, so I haven't been able to finish many of the books the nurses have given me. Whatever spare time I've had after those sessions has been lost; as soon as I stumble back to my compartment, I collapse on the couch. Once or twice River has checked on me to make sure I'm still alive, my catatonic mind suspended in other worlds while recovering from years of exhaustion and preparing for more. Most people don't get that kind of rest, ever.

I flip through the pages of *Drugsberry*. They've been severely marked up in my absence. River didn't find this while cleaning out my *cell*. More likely, someone gave it back to the library where somebody else grabbed it and took notes in the margins. She must have noticed the little book in my room at one point and pulled some strings to get it back to me.

Remembering the clock, I head toward the door and plop the book on the couch on my way out. Nostalgia can wait.

The hallways bustle with all sorts of people. Doctors, nurses, Council members, and the best botanists roam around with dark determination on their faces. They perceptibly tense up near the guards as they pass by; a simple crunch of the shoulders or flitting eyes. Others might not notice it, but I do. I've spent enough time doing it myself. The guards are the only ones with facemasks on - not all, but some of them. Us.

Their dark, beady eyes show absolutely zero emotion.

I have always avoided these hallways during their busiest times, but with the whir of people breezing around, I'm suddenly stunned by how clean the halls really are. The smell of fresh linen and the remnants of bleach linger in the air, nothing like the stale sweat and body odor I was used to. Occasionally, as a guard walks by, I catch a whiff of something awful that takes me back, but nothing as extreme as what I've experienced in the past.

Something about the bleak sterility of the area bothers me. Without people buzzing around, there would be no evidence that anyone had ever been here.

It occurs to me in a moment of horror that I'm not entirely sure where to report. I don't know where Meyer lives or what area of the complex he'll be working in today. Where do I go?

"There you are," Meyer's voice bursts from behind me, "I've been looking everywhere for you. I see you haven't gotten too far."

I turn, expecting him to be upset, but instead he looks at me with a closed-lipped smile. I wonder how he can be lighthearted during times like these. Someone nearly took his life months ago. Today could be his last day.

"Hi," I say.

The gargled sound of my voice wipes the smile from his face. He hands me a ratty olive-green jumper with a sad little shake of his head.

"You're going to want to put this on. It's probably too big. The last guy who wore it had some meat on him."

"What happened to 'im?" I ask, my eyes bulging.

"Let's just say he transferred to another division."

He leads the way and gestures to me to follow him. He fumbles around in his huge chest pocket as he walks, then brings forth a thick paper card.

"Here is your new ID Card. For every quarter of an hour of work you do, you get one minute of shower time. You're expected to work at least ten hours a day. Sometimes you may be required to work more, but you'll get more stamps for that. You submit your timecards at the end of each day and someone will enter the time onto your card. The shower room is guarded from the outside and someone will time how long you bathe for, so don't get greedy."

I do the math quickly. Forty minutes of shower time every day, maybe more? How could this possibly be true? It explains why the smells in the hallway are bearable.

"Guard this card with your life, Edwin. You only get one each year," he says, waving the card in front of my face. "Things are different on this side. We work hard, so we make sure we get rewarded and take advantage of that. That doesn't mean that there aren't thieves here. Someone sees that card just laying around, they'll snatch it," he talks quickly, "And between you and me, you can use these cards for a lot more than some spit from the faucet. People use these to buy all sorts of things; soap, food, favors, you name it. It isn't something we talk about, but these cards are gold. If you have to quit taking showers because you need to put some food in your mouth, you do it."

I nod my head at him and stare in wonder. When was the last time I'd cleaned up – and with soap, for that matter?

"You need some food, you go to Quinn. She's the only sport who'll take that card for trade without giving you a hard time."

"Thank you, Meyer," I say, amazing myself by pronouncing everything correctly.

"Sure, kid. How's speaking going?"

"Going," I respond. I follow him down the hall. Every now and then we pass by a dusty painting of something; fruit baskets, pets playing in the park, an empty water glass - the small simplicities of former everyday life that most of us won't live to experience. I recognize the crudely manufactured aluminum frames as our compound's own shoddy workmanship.

"Well, it takes time," he says. "Believe me, I've been there."

A smiling woman walks by with a tray of some kind of baked goods; tan, sweet smelling, and speckled with chocolates. The name for them escapes me. I know I've seen the name for them in a book somewhere. The entire moment feels like a dream. I pass on taking one.

"And believe me, now that you're on our side, the food gets a lot better," Meyer smiles fully this time, the corners of his eyes wrinkling. His teeth look a lot like my own, only wider and longer. "Just don't eat too much of it or you'll start looking like me. And you'll get sick if you eat too much too soon."

I can't help but smile at his joke. As we walk, our steps fall in line with each other's.

Now I remember. Cookies. They're called cookies.

"Where are we going?" I ask.

"I'm showing you to the office. It's a place you're going to get familiar with." He picks up the pace.

Various hallways are labeled with signs above their doorsills with phrases like "Greenhouse Entry 1" and "Sanitation." Everything is so organized.

I point up at the signs. "Luna Bay?" I gnarl out.

"We don't call it that here. Luna Bay to the Least Privileged is the greenhouse to us. Sanitation houses E Quadrant. You'll get used to the names."

Meyer leads us into a cramped office, monitors lining one wall. A giant calendar poised next to the entryway serves as his focus. Several letters are written on every dated square, names scribbled next to them. On today's date, two letters are missing signatures. Meyer picks a clipboard up off of a splintery desk and consults the top sheet.

"Damn it," he mumbles, "Looks like you're going to carpentry. My usual guy for the greenhouse is out with hypoxemia. We try to have a handful of people there at all times. I'm not sure the others quite know what they're into yet. They need someone with experience. I'll take over there today." He sighs.

"Sir?"

"Oh. Hypoxemia is a fancy way of saying someone has low oxygen levels in their blood. We've been having some issues with ventilation, but it's nothing to worry about. The lack of oxygen mostly makes people tired."

Something about the way he furrows his eyebrows and sighs suggests otherwise, but I simply nod. Working a dozen hours a day without oxygen? Won't that ruin productivity?

If Airlee still works in carpentry, we'll see each other again. My heart speeds up at the thought of returning, but I'm not sure what spawns my excitement more – the prospect of seeing her or the knowledge of what I did to give her away. I'll finally have a clue about what's happened to her.

"Look, I'm sorry I can't fully train you today, but you know what you're doing, right? You've seen guards in action. We do a lot of sitting around and announcing what time it is. If you're unlucky, someone might try to end you with a shard of glass, but the odds are in your favor. They'll be too focused on where you went, why you're doing what you're doing," he pauses, "And where that thing came from." He gestures at my mouth.

"If there's anything you need, you let someone know. Remember, Edwin, we live to serve, to fight through it all so we can have our day."

I look around the hallway blankly. "I don't know my way dere from here," I say, shaking my head.

"I'll show you," he replies and signals for me to follow him.

"Meya," I struggle, "you should know somethin'. Da tall guy in rehab told me he's faking."

Meyer strokes his chin. "I suppose we'll have to do something about that, won't we? I've suspected as much. Thanks, Edwin. You're a good kid."

He leads me back the way we came and to a cramped lobby. A white door presents itself starkly, looking glossy and freshly painted next to walls tanned with layers of dirt – a far cry from the cleanliness I've seen elsewhere. I stand confused for a moment; there's no knob on the door, only a thick wheel.

"Go on, turn it to the right," Meyer instructs.

I drag my feet as I move forward. He speaks to me about what time I should return to this spot on the other side of the door while I struggle to muster the strength to get it open. When I finally do, I'm shocked.

The door leads directly to the Least Privileged half of the compound. Everything seems cloaked in a shadow. I turn my head back to confirm that I'm not seeing things. It isn't the drab slate grey and patina green color scheme, but the lighting itself. They've been given less light. My feet remain firmly planted on the peeling tiles, taking it all in.

"The first time back is hard. You never realize that you were living in a cave until you leave the cave."

Two guards shove by me and form a line farther down the hall.

I sneak a look at Meyer. His face stiffens.

I step down onto the hard concrete. A draft of hot, musty air suffocates me as Meyer locks the door behind me, leaving me alone with a group of strangers. I cough as I make my way to the back of the line.

"You wanna cover that, pal?" one of the guards growls as he fidgets with his mask. I'm guessing his surgery left his face marred. Around him, others straighten out their clothing and battle the urge to close their eyes.

The guard's comment sticks for a minute, but I let it go; I need to get used to being whole, even if it makes me look like the odd one out. These moments of agony are worth the multitudes of pleasure and prosper I'll experience later. I hope. I cough again. The air is beyond stagnant.

"There it is again! Cover your mouth when you cough, you numbskull."

Oh.

Time drags on as the door opens and shuts, letting light steal its way in. Men queue up behind me in perfect formation. As the line grows too long, they form a second one. Light chatter fills my ears as people talk to their neighbors. I sweat and hope for the least amount of human contact possible.

"Where you headed?" the man next to me nudges my arm. A faded red bandana obscures his mouth.

Just my luck.

"Carpentry," I answer, taking my time to pronounce the word.

"Old Mey not up to it? No surprise there, after what happened," he rolls his eyes.

Scars mar his face. He's clearly gotten in some rough fights – at least one where someone held him down; neat blade marks streak his left cheek. As I try to imagine what might have happened, his words register. Why wouldn't Meyer be up to working in the carpentry unit?

I part my lips to ask for an elaboration, but think better of it as the hallway goes silent. Meyer looms over at us in the doorway. Lines form in his forehead. He grunts.

"Get ready, boys. We're thin today and we'll be thinner tomorrow. I'll be in the greenhouse today. You all know where to go. Everyone welcome Edwin. He's new to our little force."

Most of the eyes in the room shift in my direction. A couple of people make faces. I'm not bold enough to make any back. Maybe someday I'll feel more like a part of the team, but not right now.

Meyer nods at us and heads toward the greenhouse. The feeding alarm goes off and I panic; I haven't heard its uncomfortable screech for a long time, but it hasn't been long enough.

What if anyone's privacy is violated on my watch? Will I be able to step up and handle it tactfully?

My skin blushes just thinking about the day my mask popped off. Everyone saw my face for what it really was – a mess of bumpy skin, folds where they shouldn't be. Some people are lucky and have very little to be embarrassed about. I don't want to be part of the reason anyone becomes uncomfortable.

The door hatch flies open again and nurses file down the halls. I briefly catch a glimpse of River solemnly marching along with the others, medical bag in hand. I figured she'd be at the front of the line if anything, but it's not the case. As the stream of nurses ends, the backs of the guard lines follow them and fan out to assigned living quarters.

I follow a handful of nurses to an especially bleak part of the compound I've never seen before. Something seems off immediately. Short cells about three feet tall line the hall on both sides. One cell stands atop another, presumably to save space.

The other guards start to line the walls in no particular order, so I follow the man who spoke to me earlier. The nurse at the far end of the hall opens up the first cell's door. One by one down the line, nurses unlock and open up the little rooms. They lean their patients against the inside of the doors, where they can't be seen from my angle. Some of the nurses set up IVs. Others seem to perform examinations.

"They let *you* in here? Guess they want to put you back where you belong, after all," the man on the other side of me says, shaking his head.

I don't know how to react with anything but a glare. Instead of arguing, I focus on my job. The Council chose me to be here. Who's this stranger to say that I don't belong? *Ass-*

hole.

In front of us, a nurse with thick strawberry blonde hair unlocks a cell's door, its grey hinges squeaking. Rusty grates make up the cell's ceiling and floor. The little creature inside slides to the far-right corner and grips the grating with all of her meager strength. The nurse sighs, leans in, and wrangles her body closer to the edge of the cell.

"Olivia!" she cries in frustration, tugging away at her little frame. The girl rears up in a high-pitched whine.

It's the first sound I've ever heard come from a child.

The girl, about the age of three, tries to wiggle her way out of the nurse's arms. Her baggy burlap pants slide down a few inches with her effort. Her shirt, full of holes and covered in grime, looks like it was repurposed from an old cloth shopping bag.

However young, she's learned to fear authority already. Her eyes dart wildly around the hallway. She even tries to claw the nurse.

Yellow liquid rains down on the struggling pair seconds after the IV pierces the girl's skin. She has a mouth; I don't know why they're feeding her with an IV.

"Hold it in!" a guard yells. He bangs his fist ferociously on the top cell.

More urine flows through the ceiling grate, narrowly missing the child.

The experience. They're giving her the experience of being Least Privileged.

"I said, 'hold it in!'" the same guard bellows.

This is unlike anything I've ever seen, and I started from the bottom.

"You over there, grab some clothes from the closet and bring them to me. I'll take her feeding out here. You, see what's wrong with the one on top," the nurse orders, pulling the little girl from her cell while waste continues to fall from the ceiling.

The irate guard fumbles with the lock. Seething, he rips the door open.

The child inside peers out. Aside from some obvious malnourishment and soiled pants, he looks fine.

"I'm sorry," he mumbles. I take in a sharp breath. It's the first time I've heard a child speak. The melody of his voice catches me by surprise. "I couldn't hold it."

"Like hell you couldn't," the guard grips the boy's arms until pale white skin glows around his fingertips. "This is the fifth time in a month you've done this, and let me tell you, I'm pretty goddamn sick of it."

"I'm sorry," the boy says bashfully.

"Look at me!" the guard screams, making the boy flinch.

"You're wasting our time. You're lucky to be here, do you understand that? You should use your eyes. The grates are there for a reason."

"She won't get out of the way. I don't think she knows how to hear," the boy's face contorts with tears.

While the nurse tends to the girl, I peek into her little abode. It's nothing more than a five by three cell. The cement floor underneath the grating is caked with aged feces. I exchange a pained look with the guard standing to my left. He shakes his head almost imperceptibly and then forces himself to gaze forward, locks of blue-black hair falling in front of his eyes.

"Jesus, it's no wonder Sammy Boy puts these kids here. No sense of responsibility, just like their parents," the guard laughs, talking to the entire room. A couple of guards nod voraciously. The nurses mostly just stare.

The boy quakes in fear, his breath jagged.

I finally understand what I'm looking at. This is what happens to unapproved children. The Council makes them wait to come to a certain age before having them join the others in Bourney. Before maiming them to put them on an even level with the Least Privileged. I've always heard rumors about what happens to kids like this, but never envisioned it being this bad.

"Enjoy those precious baby teeth of yours, Carlisle. This will be your last day with them if I have my way. Bonnie, when you're finished with her, drag him to the Detention Center."

My stomach churns. These are just kids. This may be my first adult experience with them, but I was a child, too, once. I remember. I remember what it was like. It wasn't like this. It isn't reasonable to harass a five-year old.

"Give him a break, why don't you? He's just a kid," I say.

The guard grunts and whirls toward me as a nurse jabs the child with an IV.

"I have authority over punitive measures in these quarters. That's how it has been and how it always will be, newbie. If you don't like it, we can claim your mouth, too."

My jaw snaps shut. I glare at the floor for the remainder of the feeding. The Council voted for my surgery; can't they vote to spare this kid from an even more burdensome life? I can't imagine living for years physically whole and then having that taken away.

It brings up a question I haven't allowed myself the privilege to think about: who were my parents? I don't remember ever being locked in a box like this, but most of the children here are young – under six, at the oldest. Would I even remember?

I'm reminded of the stories I read as a child of lions kept in tight zoo cages, monkeys slithering between bars to escape. The animals in picture books always smiled. I don't think this child has smiled a day in his brief life, nor will he be able to if this grunt has his way.

Movement in the line thrusts me back into reality. Guards scatter in different directions as everyone heads off to their assigned workshops. I have to ask for directions to the carpentry area, earning me a raised eyebrow in the process. So much for a pleasant on-boarding process.

"What do you think you were doing back there?" a voice from behind me calls. I turn. It's the man with the red bandana.

"Turn back around," he says, "I don't want too many people to know I can speak."

"Why wouldn't you want dat?" I ask.

He sighs. "They think if you can't speak, you're some kind of idiot. I've overheard things you wouldn't believe. Things that if they knew I knew, I'd be done."

I glance to the side.

"Like what?"

"Stay quiet and I promise you'll see what I mean. We won't accomplish anything if they keep picking us off one by one."

His voice vibrates in my ear.

"Do guards not last long?" I panic. *Are my fears worth the agonizing worry, after all?*

"You misunderstand, Edwin. Anyone who tries to change anything too drastically gets decommissioned. The workers, the guards, even the leaders. Once you've awakened to the true way of our world, you can never go back," he pauses, "You're not there yet, though, are you?"

"What's your name?" I ask, suddenly aware that this could be a test.

"Ah, a suspicious one," he says mostly to himself, "Call me Sanguine."

With that, he walks away into a sea of guards and workers, many others with dark hair, wearing the same blood red bandana. In seconds, he blends in. Invisible.

I arrive at the carpentry unit with a blinding headache. Fortunately for me, the workers aren't building anything. No hammer and nails. The only weapons I have to fear are splintered old paintbrushes and the sound of twenty people's gentle brushstrokes. They're painting wooden dolls, vapid black eyes staring into the unknowable void.

While doing roll call, I check for Airlee's name and don't see it. My heart speeds up. Maybe she's been promoted; her skills were invaluable during my time here. Hardly any of the names on the list look familiar, though. The faces I do recognize seem weathered and thinner than before. Part of me expects them to ask me questions, but instead they focus on their dolls, disconcerted frowns pulling at the edges of their eyes.

Sitting around doing nothing proves to be exhausting, but it's the perfect opportunity to really take a good look around the room. As a carpentry worker, my tasks strictly revolved around production. As a result, all I truly needed to know was where the tools were located and how to complete each job. In this room as an authority figure, I find myself glancing around with newfound interest.

I look up at the cobwebbed air vents and discover a paper airplane stuck between two pipes; if I want to, I could have it removed. Fingerprinted, even. I have that power now. I walk around opening up cabinets out of curiosity, pretending to look for something, just nosing around. A few faces glance in my direction and quickly avert their gazes. I wonder which one of them was brave – and stupid – enough to launch a paper airplane.

One in particular doesn't look away, though. Her misty grey eyes size me up as I venture throughout the room. Aside from checking her name off during roll call, I have no idea who she is.

"What's ya name?" I ask, letting my "R" slip. Her eyes narrow into suspicious slits and her grip on the doll tightens just for the slightest moment.

She raises her hands with an unmistakable look of annoyance, revealing smudges of black paint – the messy and inescapable product of a long day's work – and signs the name Margeaux, a relatively common name for workers. The sickly whiteness of her skin makes her stick out prominently among the others. It's difficult to tell with the grey bandana covering her mouth, but she looks about age seventeen. It's rare for people so young to work in advanced positions like this. I wonder if this is her first post and if she was chosen for something as trifling as having small, feminine hands to handle detail work with.

Then again, I worked with one digit nearly completely missing.

"How long you been here, Margeaux?"

She pauses before answering, and then holds up a solitary finger.

"A week?"

She puts her hands together and spreads them apart as if tightening a string.

"A month?"

She nods while tilting her head. *Almost a month.*

I glance around at the glut of unfamiliar faces. Some of the workers look as though they've never learned a thing about painting in all their lives, mixing dark colors with light ones without cleaning the brush, and using giant brushes for detail work. I should really say something, but it can wait.

I keep my voice low and slow, embarrassed by my slurred speech.

"Way-uh 'as everyone gone? When I... A couple months ago, none of you wah 'ere."

The wrinkles at the corners of her eyes turn up in what I can only guess is ridicule, and her forehead turns the color of a ripe tomato as her blood pressure skyrockets. She points at me and repeats the string mime with her hands. *You were gone so long.*

"Did you know Airlee?" I ask.

Her expression goes slack. She nods.

"What happened to her?"

Margeaux closes her eyes and shakes her head. Then she closes a paintbrush in her hand and runs its plastic end across her throat.

12 / SANGUINE

"*H*ave they decided what to do with her?" Sanguine asks. He takes a puff of an old cigarette and waits for a response.

Zurie watches the wisps of smoke spiral up and up, dancing with each other on their brief journey to the Sanitation Room's ceiling.

"You know those killed people way before the viruses, right?"

"You're just mad you're not on top anymore. Didn't take as long as you thought it would."

She glares.

"Barbarian. You get a mouth and this is what you use it for." She crosses her arms and begins to turn her back to him, but thinks better of it.

"Well? What are we doing with Airlee?"

She frowns. She motions for him to pass the cigarette. He hands it to her quickly and stuffs down the pride he feels at getting her to go against her own morals. Small beginnings. She takes a puff, coughs violently, and hands it back.

"We're still keeping her in holding, but Sam is going to kill her. I can feel it."

Sanguine grimaces. "Then someone better talk him out of it," he puts the cigarette out on the floor and walks out of the room, leaving Zurie to dispose of his contraband. She stares after him, flummoxed. How could it have ever got to this point?

* * *

Sanguine taps the attending guard on his shoulder – caught napping again. "Go," Sanguine points his thumb behind him. *Take a hike.*

The Detention Center hasn't gotten any nicer since the last time he visited. Chilly, shadowy, and lonely. He doesn't imagine it can be much nicer in a cage. He sits down on a bench in front of Airlee's cell. He watches her huddled up in a corner, freezing.

"You're going to tell me everything you know about what happened – who recruited you, how you think you got caught. Then I'm going to get you a blanket and we're going to figure out how to make this right. Do you understand?"

She turns her head toward him silently, taking in her first real visitor in weeks.

She closes her eyes and nods. She starts from the beginning, never sparing a detail.

* * *

"Quinn," Sanguine eyeballs her as he walks by. He means to pass her, never mentioning a word, but he can't help himself. Although his conversation with Airlee didn't yield much, he has suspicions. He walks backward to her and sticks a menacing finger in her face. "If you *ever* rat out one of my people, say if Sam offers you a better deal, you will find yourself in a very dangerous position. Do you understand me?"

The old woman rears up and laughs at him, her hearty voice bouncing down the hallway.

"I wouldn't rat you out," she wheezes, "Maybe the other one, but who'd believe me?"

Her reaction stuns him. He didn't know about Quinn's feelings for Zurie.

"What about Airlee? Would you rat her out?" he asks.

Her eyes narrow. "Real pretty one, short?" Sanguine nods. "I almost lost my cover on that one. Sammy had a hard time identifying my face on camera. Lucky thing MacRose was able to convince him I was that ignoramus in speech therapy; the one who's been there forever. Your newbie gave him away to the Council. Good scapegoat."

"Ugh. How do you know that? Even I didn't know that," he sputters. *Makes sense he'd mix you up with that hideous mug,* he thinks as an afterthought.

"Meyer likes to talk after he's had some hooch. The lazy bastard will be executed for sure. Only a matter of when."

He relaxes his muscles. "Okay then," he says, "The good-for-nothing probably deserves it." He tosses an Identification Card in her direction. "Thanks for the information. There's more if you keep it up."

The corners of her lips twitch up in a greedy grin. She nods her head once.

He continues on his way, satisfied that Quinn hasn't jeopardized the mission.

13 / EDWIN

Airlee is dead. Airlee is dead and there's not one thing I can do to change it. It's my fault. I'll never see her again – like a speck of lint swatted out of the air, she's gone, just like that. No big announcement. Not even recognition for the hard work she'd done before turning sides. They just made her into *nothing*.

In the moment Margeaux had told me, time stopped. I simply stood there. I didn't ask what exactly Airlee had done; I had a pretty good idea. If I ask another guard about it, I'll find out, but part of me doesn't want to know.

I want to focus on the good things.

It's pretty hard to when the first friend you've ever had has been executed.

They could have tried re-educating her, sending her to therapy, de-ranking her, even. Why was violence the only viable option? No one even announced her death to make an example out of her.

I was so callous to think that she deserved whatever she had coming to her. Some of her gripes with the compound might have been valid. Maybe we could have talked about them and made the compound a better place, but she's gone now.

I rest in my compartment clutching *The Short Mysteries of Drugsberry*, staring at the popcorn ceiling while salty tears stream down my face. All of my dreams have come true, but they're not enough. Something feels missing. Wrong. I want to tell Airlee about the first time I ever laid on this sofa and the amazing surgery that has changed my life. I want her opinion on the kids I saw in the cages. I'd like to see the way she'd react to my new smile and the fresh luster of my hair. I don't really even know Airlee, but her opinion matters.

Mattered.

Those kids. Their little voices, scared and hurt and hungry, haunt me.

I make a mental note to question Meyer tomorrow. Good idea or not.

At this point, I might as well be on another planet. I'm exhausted, both mentally and physically. I'm not sure that this is the right position for me, but even if it isn't, I need to earn the right to live, even if that means denying others theirs'. I need to come to terms with the fact that I might hurt people I care about in order to survive. I dog-ear the pages of *Drugsberry* without thinking, accidentally tearing the edges of a page or two.

I wonder how things turn out for Donald Feeny. Does he find that his dream is less rosy than he originally thought it would be? I'm always too tired to read, so I might not ever know. In a sleepy haze, I see the words "rebellion," "Zurie," and "fight" written in the margins, along with a variety of coded message, but I can't bring myself to care. I need a glass of water and I can't even muster the energy to get up to grab one.

I've already gotten one decent person killed. I'm not ready to jump to help kill another.

* * *

My one wish as the alarm blasts is to sleep underneath the safety of my warm blankets, away from the rest of the ugly world – or, at least, this microscopic portion of it. My heart sinks to the pit of my stomach imagining what horrors I'll encounter today and knowing how I'll be expected to react to them.

I sigh. It's a relief to push all of that pressure out at once. As I inhale, though, the worries somehow seem to find their way back in.

Every job is difficult starting out. Someone slit their wrist and died right in front of me on my first day at work in the glass shop. It took weeks to mentally recover from that. Throughout my time there, I learned to deal with the culture of that unit – it consisted of angry, unambitious men, and the way of life was to look at the ground or over your shoulder. My first day in the carpentry unit went much more smoothly; no one died, for starters, but I still had no clue what I was doing.

I scrape myself up off the couch and get ready for the day. Maybe I didn't leave the best first impressions with some people, but I can try to make up for it today. I might learn something new to give me a greater sense of purpose and perspective. Who knows? If I don't get up off of this couch –

If I don't get up off of this couch, a lot more will happen to me than never finding out. I could lose my compartment, my status, my mouth, my life. Any number of other terrible things could happen. Facing the day is simply accepting the idea – with an unreasonable amount of optimism – that something bad *might not* happen to me today.

But only if I get up.

* * *

"Good morning," Samuel's flat voice says over the intercom. "Thank you for another day of hard work. To accomplish our goals, we must work together in peace. I urge you to resist the temptation to follow those who lead you with false promises. Those who work hard shall be rewarded under my care, a promise that Rebels cannot live up to. Now, please rise for the Vow."

I'm standing in a lab room. The scientists in the adjoining room stare out of a plate glass window at me and my companion. The scientists reach their arms out to us and we reach ours out back.

Samuel's tired voice begins:

"I solemnly vow to support the United Army in its effort to combat all evils, to shed all darkness, and make room for the light. No contribution is too great or too small. I vow to work at my hardest for as long as I may live, and support my brethren in their own efforts for the hope of a better tomorrow."

The intercom clicks off. Not the most inspiring Vow Samuel's ever given.

This morning's routine started similarly to yesterday's – feed the young prisoners, then report to a work unit. Today, we head to the lab. Meyer's guy explains to me briefly that this is where surgeries occur, but only rarely. The compound lacks the resources to regularly perform complicated operations, explaining why so many people still lack critical parts. Normally, the lab is used for harmless experimentation. Hopefully one day, the operations won't be necessary.

Our technicians aren't even the ones who perform surgeries; some short man from another compound completes the procedures, passing in and out of our home via an airlock. River often accompanies him, pausing his work every couple of minutes to ask a question. "He looks pretty worn out when he's done," my companion laughs.

The "deformities," he labels them, are caused by war chemicals that have affected births for generations. No news to me. Some people are born completely intact, but that's rare, too. It's a promising sign for humanity, though; maybe it will take a few more generations to weed out the mutated genes, but it's possible for things to go back to normal someday. That future seems so distant, though; it's hard to imagine.

"They probably fix a guy in here once a month. Every two or three, some pregnant lady pops one out. She usually don't make it if she's from the other side. Labor's kinda hard when you ain't got no mouth. Anyway, we take the baby away and raise it in a nursery until it's of speaking age. Then we keep it in the cages if the parents weren't approved to have kids. You've gotta be on the Big List to have kiddos. Normally, they poke you and prod you to make sure you're not gonna have one with an arm coming out of its head, then match you up with the best genetic fit. You've got to be married to have one, though, even if you end up with a stranger's baby. It is *bizarre*, I'm telling you."

"Why lock da kids up?" I ask.

"Put them in their place," he shrugs. "They've got trouble in their genes; gotta tamp that out while they're young. Anyway, you may not realize it, but we've got population limits. We can't waste the best resources on genetic misfits. If they make it, they join the workers."

"What about da parents?" I say.

He leans against a pole and ponders my question for a moment. "Well," he begins, "I suppose it don't matter much what the parents think. They're giving us a problem by forcing another mouth to feed on us, but it's not the kids' faults. Potential matters most; that's why you got the new face you do. You're smart. Me? I grew up in those cages, waiting for workers to die so my name could move up a list. I never had a chance in life, yet here I am."

"You made your own chances," I reply slowly, "Otherwise you wouldn't be here."

We stand behind the glass and watch the scientists in their ratty, white lab coats rush gracefully around the small space. I think about lying on the table on the other side of the room and can't connect myself to that moment in the operating room. It wasn't terribly long ago, but it feels like another life – close to fictional, even.

My companion speaks up next to me. "I wasn't supposed to

remember being raised in the cages. The doctor we bring in specializes in child therapy. He does his best to make everyone forget – works better on the younger ones. Memory implantation," he laughs sarcastically, never once looking at me. "They once had a program that tried to trick you into thinking you were sitting under an apple tree. The goal was to make you *feel* the bark and smell the juice. It didn't work very well," he rambles. I observe the scientists in silence. The lights in the room buzz steadily.

"Hey man, I gotta take a leak. You keep them outta trouble," my companion says, his face brightening up a bit. He gently nudges my elbow and exits the room, letting the door slam behind him.

Stuck behind the soundproof glass alone, I take the time to visually probe the lab. Beakers of chemicals and boxes with assorted labels line shelves neatly screwed against the walls. It's the brightest, most organized space I've seen in the entire facility.

The two scientists chat to each other inanimately as they hover over some worksheets and a vast selection of glass dishes. Their conversation gains a little vigor as they appear to argue about something. I sigh out of boredom, lean forward, and prop my head up on my hand, accidentally hitting a button on the control panel. I hear a faint click. Their voices erupt on my side of the glass.

"— Wouldn't have to do this if Sam let the kids go," one of them says.

"They wouldn't be there if their parents were smart enough to keep their legs closed," the other retorts, "Anyway, ninety-five percent of them are orphans. We engineer a couple babies, the population evens out."

"The kids' lives don't matter because someone else screwed up?"

The other scientist exhales loudly. "I've heard rumors that Sam is trying to do away with the children's prisons. River has been training with the Barclay doctor, too. Soon those kids could be free, integrating with the rest of the rats."

A moment passes by. What's taking my partner so long? Not that I mind – the longer the better. Seems like this could get interesting.

"For your information, we're not breaking even with the population. We're not even logging this shit anymore!" The first scientist glares at his co-worker.

"Passion Fruit, Apple Blossom, whatever her name is? She'll make a great match with the guy who tried to slice Meyer's balls off. Their kid will be hot *and* feisty." He shuffles some papers on the table.

"Too bad you won't be alive to see her come of age, Vince."

"Yeah, whatever. She's not going to have a mouth and that's half the fun."

"You're sick, man," the other scientist raises an eyebrow. "Really twisted."

"Not like that, dude. I like to argue with my women; ours can't even talk. Sam tells us to flip a switch and we just *do* it. Can you imagine falling for someone whose voice you can't even hear?"

I scratch my head as I consider their banter. I've never thought about my parentage before now; everything has been about just living and getting ahead. I didn't know that the compound even could make babies outside of traditional means. I run my hands through my hair. Was I a... test tube baby? Or was I one of the kids in the cages? Workers don't get approved to have children; there aren't many other possibilities.

Why would scientists make a baby that doesn't have a mouth? Maybe they can't just "turn off" genes to fix mutations.

"You know Sam's considering alternate disabilities?" Vince continues. "Instead of making them not have mouths, he wants us to experiment with eyes, hearing. He thinks it'll boost production if they have a harder time communicating with each other. My problem is," he goes on, "that we can't go off message without making people think something's up. They'll ask why there are new deformities."

"It wouldn't be the first time. Last time we blamed the water," the other scientist responds.

My body goes numb. *Instead of making them not have mouths...* My people don't just have mutations. The Most Privileged are maiming us before we even take our first breaths. The air in the room seems to grow stale as my heart races.

"The Barclays make some of their people sick on purpose. They say it makes the healthy ones feel like their contribution matters more. Half their pain can be turned off with the right drugs, but they won't do it. Their surgeon talks a lot when you give him whiskey."

It just keeps on getting worse.

"We're only doing our part so we can get what's ours," Vince plunges a pipette into a beaker and mindlessly squirts and sucks the liquid within it.

"If we had the resources, we could save everyone from those thieves."

"Look, man, stop thinking about it. Stay positive. If we pair these genes right, we can give someone a chance at a better life than they'd have with someone else doing this job. *We* would never pair our girl with Hairy Thomas, for example," he pauses for emphasis, "We've been doing this for *years*."

"Way too long. I can't help but feel like we're adding to the problem. If we didn't make them their fancy stuff, maybe they'd realize they *need* our help. Maybe they'd feed us."

"Probably a lot more likely that we'd die. They'd just get their stuff from someone else."

The door clicks behind me as my companion walks back in. I lift my arm and pretend to scratch the back of my head. He starts speaking just as the intercom shuts off.

"What's the matter? You look like you seen a ghost," he says.

I purse my dry lips together. To be alone would be paradise, but in this world, paradise either exists in your head or not at all.

He steps forward, revealing a hunched figure behind him.

"You remember this little guy from yesterday? The surgery got approved. Someone caught me on my way back and handed him off." My companion shifts uncomfortably.

How could someone approve a surgery to maim a child? Especially when we don't have the resources to correct everyone.

I lean toward the boy. If I hadn't been so distracted, I know I would have smelled him before I saw him. He reeks of dried fecal matter and urine, the stale sweat produced by a compact living space pouring off of him like too many sprays of foul cologne. He'd been given absolutely no real chance at life.

Who, exactly, approved this?

Ignoring his putrid smell and soiled body, I lean further down and do my best to smile.

"You dun half anything to be afraid of. I used to have no mouf. You can't talk. You can't eat. A lot will change, but you'll go on," I say, tapering off quickly.

The child stares at me blankly, clearly not comforted. In my case, surgery improved my quality of life. Not so for him.

My companion draws the boy forward through a heavy door and into the lab with the two scientists. A third man with yellowing skin arrives from a side door, greets the boy, and waves him into another room. It occurs to me that the term "corrective surgery" can have multiple meanings depending on who you're talking to.

Turning my emotions off would be an amazing skill right now. Instead, my entire body feels hollow.

My companion returns to my side of the room.

"How often does dis happen?" I ask.

"The reversals? Ain't often," he pauses, "We do more surgeries doing things like olfactory suppression, hearing removal."

I stare blankly.

"They remove your sense of smell," he answers.

"How do you put up with dis?" I dare to ask.

"It's simple. You'll get it, Edwin. You will. If you want a good life – food, water, a decent place to sleep – you're going to have to do some things you don't want to do and see a lot more you don't wanna see. If I won't do these things, someone else will," he pauses in reflection, "Maybe that makes me an immoral man, maybe stupid or shortsighted. Every time I look at those kids, though, I'm reminded of where I came from and where I am now. It's the last place I want to go back to."

A quiet moment passes.

"I want to help him. Really. But who's going to help you and me?"

He's right. Why interfere when someone would just stop us and take all three of our mouths?

If only he knew the real reason people are born deformed. It's not bad DNA, contaminants in the food, chemical residue, or any of the other stories we've been trained to believe. It's us. We've deformed ourselves. We let it happen.

I open my mouth to speak, but can't bring myself to actually do it.

The rest of our time in the little room passes in a silent blur, one racing thought leading to the next.

14 / AIRLEE

*A*irlee sits in the Detention Center cell trying her best not to weep, and ultimately failing miserably. *If he hadn't taken an interest in me, I wouldn't be here. He ratted me out. He ruined everything.*

The icy cement floor makes the pads of her toes swell and that's only the beginning of her grievances; the toilet seat is so grimy and caked with crust, it can't have been scrubbed for years. She's thought of crouching on it to avoid touching the lid, but the notion of showing her captors that they've succeeded in making her uncomfortable makes her want to throw up. Anyway, she doesn't have the strength to rebel.

If I barf, she thinks, *they've really succeeded. No need to worry about an execution. Clean hands.*

There were no kinks in her plans to explore the Rebellion's ideals up until meeting Edwin. She and Quinn had access to the library and wrote messages to each other in its aged pages, at first making a game of it as they grew to know each other. The messages became far more serious as time wore on. The whole thing was silly. Of course the library would have cameras, plain-clothes guards, *something* to cause the Council to disregard her side of the case. They found messages she'd left directly for Zurie.

Or maybe, as she suspected, Edwin had snitched on her, and that was enough.

Whatever the case, uncovering the means of her discovery won't free her. The jail's thick, rusty bars see to that. Anyway, she's sure that the Most Privileged have declared her guilt, and she has nowhere to run to.

"We have physical evidence of your plots against us, Airlee," said Samuel vaguely during their sole, brief meeting, "and I'm not sure what to do with you in the meantime. You've proven yourself a traitor, but a cunning one. We might be able to use that someday if you change your mind a little. While we decide on your fate, you'll sit and reflect in our Detention Center. You're a lucky woman for a guard to not have taken matters into his own hands."

"Yes," a redhead among the Council sneered, "a guard would have crushed you."

The meeting plays in her mind constantly, each word turned upside down and backward in a desperate search for greater meaning. "We've gotten quite a bit more strict lately," he'd said.

Did this mean she could die for her harmless little messages? Sure, she and the cook had talked about what it would take to escape, but they had never discussed actually attempting it.

It was on her agenda, though. She wonders what exactly exists on the outside of the compound – what the people are like, mostly.

Not that she'd leave the exit a secret at this point.

She's sat freezing in this cell for weeks, mulling everything over in her mind. Why is she here and not Quinn? Have they executed her?

She remembers the day the guards stormed into the carpentry shop to arrest her. In her hands she'd held an oversized wooden stool as she inspected a particularly ugly mahogany stain that the mousy guard on duty instructed her to apply. At the sound of footsteps, he turned toward the door, Airlee's side of the room, and back to the door again. Airlee raised an eyebrow at Margeaux, her new benchmate. Someone was coming.

Her first thought was of Edwin and if the grimy man oozing through the door was responsible for his promotion. Or death. She'd heard rumors about both.

For a while, guards told everyone that he moved up the

ranks and would no longer live with the Least Privileged, but Airlee wasn't so quick to believe that. After all, they had said the same thing about her mentors. The guards offered no proof of their claims. Friends and family would at least try to visit or find a way to send a note, wouldn't they? Airlee and Quinn weren't the only ones who had devised methods of cross-communication.

After the guards had had enough of everyone's conspiracy theories and inquiries, they'd started walloping on anyone daring enough to reach out. No one bought Samuel's morning speeches, the glorious half-truths he spat out every day to motivate manic masses. After about a week, people stopped asking about him.

Margeaux caught Airlee's expression just as the rest of the group pressed in. Five guards total. Airlee lowered her stool with a *thunk*.

"Airlee?" one grunted. Of the men who came, only this one could speak.

She turned her head reflexively toward the doorway. The men must have seen a picture of her. A brief scan around the room was all it took before the gruff titan who called for her gripped her arm and ripped her off her own stool, knocking over another worker in the process. Airlee fought to communicate with him to get him to stop, but he dragged her ruthlessly across the floor in spite of her attempts.

Despite exploring the ideologies of a violent group of people, she was not a violent person. Maybe, given a more humane approach, she would have gone willingly, but this was no interrogation. The seriousness of the situation iced over her, paralyzing her for a second, until the next thing she knew her fists had balled up and flailed wildly. She never once connected with anything but dry air, but she didn't have much time to try.

The tension in the air was palpable; remembering it makes Airlee's hands quake with anxiety. The worker who had been knocked over jumped up, furious, but the first to intervene in the assault wasn't him or even Margeaux.

Workers watched Airlee's feral eyes as the guard began pulling her by a fistful of hair. She tried to rise to her feet to avoid the pain of being dragged from behind like a heavy bag of trash. It took about thirty seconds for someone's rage to boil over. A sinewy man with ashy blonde hair sprang to her rescue, tapping the guard's shoulder to get his attention.

The guard whipped his arm across the worker's face without even looking at him and all Hell broke loose; the blonde's bench mates, hardened workers with three decades of combined experience, catapulted forward and battered the guard with their bare fists.

An older woman rammed the remaining members of the group with the unstained seat of the stool she'd been working on. Another man waited for an opening and smashed the edge of his stool into the head of the guard dragging Airlee.

Her head cracked against the rock-hard floor as he staggered and let go. Warmth trickled down her crown as she lay on the floor feeling defeated in spite of her momentary freedom. She wasn't strong enough to fight back, and was now unable to join in. Her vision went black for a few seconds and her ears rang like sirens – however this ended, she wasn't going anywhere on her own now.

Airlee's bench mates rushed to her. Prone on the floor, bleeding, the worst seemed possible; she had fallen hard. They dragged her to a dusty, unused corner and propped her up. *Everyone will take a turn fighting by the time this is over,* she thought.

She witnessed the full uproar of the room from her new perspective, even as her sight faded in and out. One guard lay on the floor face down, completely still, blood pooling around his head. Another, red ooze flowing down the right side of his face, looked around the room in a panic before fleeing to the hallway. Someone hummed an unopened can of paint at his back. It slammed into his shoulder blade with a strange, hollow *thwack* and he collapsed against the door before scampering out.

Someone else decided an unopened can wasn't good enough – she had already pried the lids off of several fresh ones, waiting for the right moment. The remaining three guards had whipped out their batons in between flurries of flying wrenches and didn't see the woman's arms surge up to splash them in the eyes. They stumbled back down the hall and tried to wipe away the navy blue liquid with their fingers, further blinding themselves.

Their injured officer hunched his back and moved as fast as his body could carry him. No one could call for help. The workers took out the one who could speak first. His blood continued spreading across the floor. A dent grooved the right side of his skull.

More guards would arrive in minutes, so everyone worked together to shut the door, lock it, and barricade it with every moveable object they could find. Never having truly worked as a team before, most seemed to enjoy the process – handing each other objects, tending to each other's wounds, congratulating each other for their standup morals and quick thinking – even in spite of leaving bloody footprints all over the floor.

For others, the rage never quelled. Everyone expressed it differently. Some smashed benches. Others wrote obscenities all over the walls:

Kill Sam. Fuck the Barclays. Fuck you.

Others kicked the corpse, taking sick pleasure with each and every crack of a rib. For Airlee, it was enough to make her wish the War had wiped humanity out and been done with it.

Someone behind her sprayed a chemical to the wound on her head. She winced. The person started to bandage the gash in a rush, maintaining pressure to staunch the bleeding.

"You didn't do anything wrong," a familiar voice said.

She turned in confusion. In the chaos that enveloped the room, she forgot about the guard actually assigned to their work unit. He had been with them for about two weeks, having substituted in the shop before.

Tears bubbled over Airlee's eyes and she struggled to breathe. Because of her, this brave man would pay the ultimate price for doing what he thought was his job. No one had told him that his guardianship applied to inanimate assets only, not to justice or self-defense or even the safety of others. Hostile workers could be replaced. Airlee didn't think his creative view on the situation would pan out well for him.

As she sat there bleeding, surrounded by people who would certainly be executed, the doubts she had about the compound solidified. What was there for her to aspire to? She could never treat someone like an animal.

Maybe her next life would be sunnier, but she'd had hopes

for this one. She'd hoped the fire she had in her heart – along with so many others – would burn their institutions down, but thus far, she'd only gotten hosed.

She fought the sting in her eyes as she wondered about the value of her life. Margeaux might miss her a little, but other than her, no one would care if she died. This riot wasn't about just her.

It was that moment there on the floor – her vision fading in and out before she finally lost consciousness – that she decided firmly where her allegiances lied.

15 / AIRLEE

*M*etal hinges screech as someone enters through the one and only door to the Detention Center. *Someone could light this whole place up and I'd have no way to escape,* Airlee thinks bitterly. Despite only seeing silent nurses and guards for days, she finds herself wishing that this looming creature would just go away. She sees the shadow and refuses to raise her head.

"What's the matter, sweetie?" the figure asks. It's a familiar voice. She saunters up to the grungy bars and wraps her fingers around them. "I'm afraid I have bad news for you. The Council approved an execution. Come the day after tomorrow, you'll just be another name thrown around history classes. They'll call you a terrorist." Her voice is genuinely warm despite her message. Soft.

Airlee tilts her head up and can't believe her eyes; she knows this woman! She tries to read her face for a lie, but finds herself distracted by something as simple as her hair.

The lights cast a white, vaguely angelic veil around her head. *This place is messing with my brain,* she thinks.

Airlee points at her and moves one hand along in a wave.

"You did ask for me," she smiles, "Here I am."

Airlee tilts her head in confusion.

She whips out a pen and notepad and chucks them into the cell. "I want to talk to you. I know you can handle writing. Hear me out. We can help each other."

Airlee bends over the small, stained notepad, her eyes trained on her new friend. She picks the pad up with her left hand and hovers over the pen with her right.

What did you do with my friend? Airlee writes, then sticks the spiral band of the notebook through the bars.

"Which friend? Quinn?"

Airlee nods and balls up her fists. Her knuckles ache – not from the beating she'd gotten a week ago, but from the constant chill. The first signs of arthritis. She hasn't told anyone for fear of being considered a nuisance.

"Your friend is alive and well. Thriving, actually. You see, while everyone thinks she chops up celery, she does no such thing. She barters for goods and information. She sold you out, the same way she sold four more people like you out today alone. For the right price, she'd probably give the Rebellion details they could use to assassinate someone with. She doesn't care. It's all trade," she shrugs delicately.

How could I have not been more careful? Airlee thinks. She studies the floor and begins to shake with anger.

"You never even met her in person, did you? If you had, you'd have known."

Airlee jots another question down on the paper.

Who else did she try to get in trouble?

"I couldn't even tell you the names on her list. She seeks out anyone at risk of creating a *disturbance*. Used to be that she helped the Rebellion recruit people. Hack," she coughs.

Airlee stares blankly at her odd visitor. Before Quinn had made her acquaintance, Airlee was a model worker. She'd labored in several shops in her life, always striving to become the best and eventually move on to a more favorable position.

Sometimes in her quest for better things, she'd been denied opportunities. The Council always claimed something; she didn't have enough experience, she was too old or too young, she didn't have a Certificate of Knowledge – even if she knew the job better than veterans. She'd done well – better than her peers – but was still held back.

She'd discussed the issue with Margeaux once before. After asking for her opinion, she'd pointed to Airlee, swiped a hand over her face, and puffed out her belly. *They think you're pretty and that you'll just get pregnant.*

Neither of them had ever seen a female guard before. Airlee had always hoped her career path would take her in that direction, but it never seemed likely to happen. *There's always nursing, but I'd rather be chained up forever,* Airlee thought.

Quinn took advantage of the way she felt about her track in life to target her. How many other women has she backstabbed?

I never meant to cause a disturbance, Airlee writes.

"You did and you didn't. We know you tried to recruit Edwin, among others, whether you realized it or not. You're a very bright girl, but even the best of us make mistakes. You were seen on camera. The Council will refute anything you say. You *will* be executed for the crime of conspiring against authority."

So, it wasn't Edwin who ratted me out. Why are you here? Just to tell me that I'm going to die?

"No. I'm on your side."

Why would you help me? she asks.

"It's always been smoke and mirrors, but now everything's going up in flames. It can't be hidden anymore. The inequality, the lack of decision-making we all have... Why is it that I have a better life than yours when we're both working for the same thing? Why should you not be given a chance from the start? If we take the correct steps, we can destroy every single immoral structure of this compound. If you agree to help, I can try to guarantee your safety," she pauses, "I'll hide you, at the very least."

Airlee flinches and moves to hand the pen and notepad back, but finds the bars blocked. She steps closer to Airlee.

"Tell me what you're thinking. I can tell you want change. I need to talk to someone who has the same kind of thoughts that I do." The desperation reigns clear in her eyes.

I don't know what to think. The guards abuse us. We're worked to death. I have another ten to twenty years of life, if I'm lucky. The only sky I've ever seen was in a children's book and a lot of workers don't even have access to those. I used to live by the motto "Help others to help yourselves," but now my only motivation to live is to leave this place. I don't care if you tell me that's impossible.

She pauses in thought, unsure if she wants to write the rest of what she's thinking.

I wouldn't be surprised if the Rebellion is all a ploy to distract us from what's really going on over there. She shoves the notebook back out of the cell.

She takes her time to contemplate Airlee's lengthy message. No one will disturb their meeting, not with a member of the Council in the room. She twists a silver bracelet around her wrist while she thinks.

"The only way to escape your chains is to remain in them for as long as you can stand it, and longer after that, until we figure out how to make permanent changes. In these last months there have been massive attacks all throughout this place, leading to executions on *both* sides. Fights over things like food and supplies are only the start. I don't even want to talk about the suicide rate. This is a small civil war now. I say this not to anger you, but think of the consequences of that. Production has gone way down. Even my people have less food. If we can't function as a society..." she trails off, deciding better on her train of thought. "We can't fight this with violence. Please try to understand where I'm coming from."

Airlee raises an eyebrow.

"I will tell you all I can in our time together, but you must promise me to listen."

I could do that, Airlee writes before thinking of her next question, *What's in it for me?*

"A greater purpose in life or death? I can't release you yet. I'll do it as soon as I can get you away without being seen."

Fine. Tell me everything you know.

"I'll start now. But like I said, I'll need you to do something for me eventually. Everyone in the Rebellion does."

16 / RIVER

"River Stone, please report to the security room immediately," the intercom blares, "I repeat: River Stone, please report to the security room *immediately* for a... code 86."

What in the world could this be about now? River thinks as she sips a cup of already cold tea. The aromatic leaves are supposed to relax her, but instead the opposite always ends up happening; the tea is hard to come by and even harder to sit still to enjoy. Her blood pressure rises as she launches out of her office in the direction of the security room, muttering under her breath.

Halfway there, she slows her pace; if the call for her truly were an emergency, the whole place would be running around aimlessly. She yawns deeply as she breezes through the familiar passageways, waving occasionally, watching people do their jobs and conduct their business.

"What's going on?" River asks as she turns the corner into

the bleak security room, trying her best to seem cheery. Sam stands behind Amy, the teenage girl who paged her. Although manning the security room isn't her official job, it's a stepping-stone to something more meaningful.

Sam mutters something unintelligible to himself. River waits impatiently, struggling to keep her composure in her irritable mood.

"The oxygen levels just took a sudden nose dive, but I can't see any reason for it aside from these outside vents," Sam points to an ancient computer monitor. "What could be causing that?"

"We've had problems because of weather before. You remember the mold issues we had years ago and how many people got sick trying to fix it. Some maintenance people found another huge patch a few days ago," River says, her face sinking, "so we have that to look forward to again. Could be that and other debris clogging the system."

"I'm not talking about that. You don't see these levels, River? Look at them! The vents must've been torn to shreds!" Sam lays his fist down among a pile of papers cluttering the desk.

River looks down and purses her lips.

"Amy, do you mind stepping out, please?" River asks. The girl doesn't need to hear what comes next. She has plenty of years ahead to worry about the compound's state of affairs. "We need ten minutes."

Amy nods her head and glides from her tattered computer chair to the exit, happy to oblige. She shuts the door with a gentle click on her way out.

River's eyes cut through her partner. "Cute. Seriously, the fist slam? Really becoming of a leader. Look, I don't need to worry about what's going on outside if there's a perfectly logical reason."

"The oxygen could be anything. There was a storm last night. We're going to have to deal with that and seal off the room I think the breach is in," Sam opens his hands repeatedly, his tone changing, "but you didn't get the code? Code 86?"

It takes River a minute. "Oh. Oh! We talked about this three years ago, I didn't remember..."

"I didn't think you would," he shakes his head and grabs her hand and holds it. She takes a deep breath.

"This is really happening?"

He nods. "They sent a messenger earlier this morning."

The room begins to spin; River clutches the back of a chair while taking a seat.

"Is that all we know?" she breathes, her eyes the size of saucers.

"They're taking twenty-five people," he whispers.

"The Barclays can't do that," she protests, "Don't they understand that we'll produce even less now?"

"That might be the case," he says, "But it relieves us of a burden. Less people to feed, more energy for everyone else. The Barclays insist we owe them something."

"Who are they taking? How are they even going to transport them?"

Sam shrugs. "There's not much I can do, unless I want to provoke ourselves into starvation. They're picking people at random. Their messenger said something about a safe vehicle. That's all I know."

"There's no way they have twenty-five suits. Our people could *die* out there! What else aren't you telling me? There's something. I can feel it."

The space goes silent. Nothing but the hum of old technology fills the room. River takes a deep breath and continues.

"What if the Barclays are sabotaging us so they get more out of the government? What if they're corrupting the vents to slow us down, and then take our people?"

"It's possible," Sam nods solemnly. He hates lying to his wife, but he must play his part when necessary.

"Sam, they make their own people deathly sick just to keep them in line! They make their people go outside, and look at how ill most of them are! We can't let them take anyone!

Tears form in her eyes.

"Do we do any different? Honestly? As hard as we've tried, the Council can't agree to be humane." Deep lines form depressions in his forehead. He rubs his temples.

"They could take me," she looks around the room aimlessly and tries to catch her breath. Sam takes her other hand in his.

"They come tomorrow morning," he says softly, "Hide. Go to the basement and stay there until nightfall."

After years of living underground, the idea of being able to discern night's arrival without seeing outside seems odd, but she thinks she can do it. "What about you?"

"They won't take me," he says, "They'd risk too much having to establish a relationship with a new leader. They won't do that."

River blinks hard. A question forms in the back of her mind. *Did he say...?*

A massive alarm interrupts her thought. Sam groans in protest as the lights flicker out and a generator powers on with a rumble. The backup lights barely illuminate the room. River rushes over to the door and thrusts it open.

The situation in the hallway is the same, emergency lights posted near the ceiling blinking an eerie crimson red. Other people rush out of their offices to inquire about the alarm, but no one knows what has happened. In the security room, the monitors remain black.

Sam heaves a sigh and rises. He nearly trips over his own feet as he joins the crowd in the hallway. Mad rushes of people converge by the main hatch.

Loud bangs and hurried footsteps come from the other side of the compound, headed in their direction – muffled, but audible enough to cause a panic. It's usually impossible to hear anything from the other side.

"What should we do?" River asks.

"The doorways dividing us seal during emergencies. We need to manually override the system to get the doors open."

"What? We don't even know who's out there!" a stranger shouts.

River nods her head at Sam. True, they don't know what's going on or who may be banging on the hatch, but at some point, the alarm must be shut off and all the doors must be opened. If anyone is hurt, there's no way to tend to them through locked doors.

"We can't just leave our people out there. Is anyone here an engineer?" Sam bellows.

A teenage boy sprints in the opposite direction. He drags back his father a short moment later; their like faces give the relationship away. They're one of the few true families in the compound and the only people of full Spanish descent. The boy's mother had died a few years back, but loved her husband and son in ways that made her family the envy of the compound.

"Milan, thank you for helping with this. We could use someone with your talent," Sam says in a rush, shaking the engineer's hand while simultaneously leading him to the control room.

"My pleasure," Milan says. Although he's always had the ability to speak, the man is soft-spoken and terse.

His son looks on helplessly – eyes wide like a lost critter – as the pair disappears into the throng. His pride in his father's engineering skills knows no bounds. He's certain that if anyone can override the locks, his father can.

"Dios mío," Milan sighs. He strokes his black beard in deep thought; he has never seen so many buttons and wires in one place before, paths totally lost in the tangled mess. Sweat creeps down Samuel's neck.

"What do you think? Can you get those doors open?" he pleads.

"It's going to be difficult, but with the right tools and a manual, I think I can manage," Milan answers, his face stone hard as he studies the panel.

"Unfortunately, we don't have a manual. You're on your own for this one," Samuel says. A nervous smile hits his face.

Milan nods, purposefully avoiding Samuel's direct gaze. Of course there would be no manual during an emergency. He crushes the grip of a screwdriver in his hand, holding back every urge to throw the damn thing.

"Can you at least get me a lantern, then?"

Samuel mutters an "oh" as if he should have thought of that before. He rummages through a stuffed cabinet. Its contents spill out onto the chalky floor. He picks up a fat red flashlight, waves it in Milan's direction, and turns it back to himself to press the 'on' button.

Nothing happens. He sighs and draws the flashlight closer to his face, awkwardly opening up the battery chamber in the dark. The four little AA batteries inside have long been corroded, the expiration date fully covered with white gunk. *We should have had a plan for an event like this,* Sam thinks, *it's not very likely there are good batteries around.*

Milan spins around and grumbles unintelligibly. What else could happen to make a difficult job harder? He begins working on the wiring under Samuel's heated observation.

"Sam!" River shouts repeatedly as she shoves her way into the entrance. He doesn't respond until he sees her in the doorway, puffing away; he stares at her dumbly, waiting for her to catch her breath.

"The oxygen levels dipped another half a percent. We need

to send someone now," she sputters.

"Send Sanguine," he orders. Milan ignores them, focusing instead on a bunch of black wires in his hand.

"I have a better idea," River begins, "What about the girl? Her time is limited. Code 86?" She suggests. They could blame the incoming group on her disappearance instead of taking the fall themselves.

"Sending her outside is execution," Sam thinks out loud, "But 86 could help us."

"Is it execution, though? You seemed pretty sure we had a storm last night. I didn't hear thunder. No one has talked about it."

His features remain flat, square. He hardly even seems annoyed by what she might be suggesting. It's enough to make her continue.

"These secretive meetings? I don't buy them anymore."

He shifts his feet back and forth between Milan and River as if deciding which matter to attend to. He finally bounces off of his left foot in River's direction, promising Milan that he will return as soon as he can. Milan waves him off, certain he can't help, anyway. Sam hands off his flashlight to a passive observer leaning against the doorway and walks with River down a hallway for some privacy.

She looks at him glumly, "You think I never suspected you

go outside? You carry yourself differently when you come back from your meetings. You even *smell* different. Someone was bound to catch on. "

He stands there dumbfounded. "How did you know?"

"I found a few dandelion seeds stuck to your pants the other morning," she looks down, "There's no way they could've gotten there unless you don't actually wear the suits. I've found a feather under your shoe before, but I gave you the benefit of the doubt. I thought it could have been from a blanket or something."

His silence in the hallway begins to discomfort her, so she keeps talking. "We need to fix the problem. Maybe the air outside isn't poisoned, but without oxygen, we die."

Samuel picks violently at his cuticles. "It wouldn't be the worst way to go, having seen some sunshine. Some of us would kill to go like that."

River agrees. "Airlee's pretty pissed at us right now, but I think she'd do it." She presses her hand to his forearm.

"She's going to die, anyway," Sam says. He places his hand on her shoulder and rubs gently, as if his smooth touch could massage her distrust of him away. Blotches of red veins spot the whites of his exhausted eyes.

"You can't be serious," she balks, "Look, I get it. People will call her a hero if they find out she's rescued the air, so we'll tell people she's dead. Where have all the other volunteers gone? The non-criminals? Why are they *really* gone?"

"If she ever escaped the basement, we'd be screwed. Escort her outside, tell her you'll bring her back in, and don't," he grumbles, "If we're lucky, a break will spark something on our end," he scratches his head. He already has one foot pointed back to the control room.

"You're not going to answer me, Sam?"

"No," he says and walks away.

Because they're dead, she guesses. But who would do that?

It suddenly occurs to her that his reason for keeping people locked inside the compound isn't because of poison at all. Anyone who has ever left has died, their bodies unrecoverable. He's always blamed hungry animals, but if she has to take a stab at why he's really so adamant about roping people indoors...

It's the Barclays.

She watches his head bob in the distance as he walks, unsure if she loves him more for his twisted sacrifice, or despises him for it.

But that's it. It's up to her. She turns, open-mouthed, and heads in the opposite direction.

* * *

Her small to-do list returns to her mind, although she

doesn't feel like completing most of it at this point. Her mind is on Airlee and the days of healing waiting for her on the other side of the hatch. There are several items she needs to pick up in preparation, but she figures she might as well grab a couple personal items while she's around Quinn. No sense in dealing with her twice.

Chocolate and toilet paper. That's all.

Like much of everything else in the compound, sweets are rare; chocolate, however, is exceedingly so. The Barclays ship small amounts of it in with their rations from time to time, pushing prices through the roof; the supply never meets the demand. River fell in love with it the first time she tried it at a small gathering. Now she hoards it in a drawer in her bedroom, waiting for the moment a craving hits to put a dent in the plastic baggy. *It could be a worse addiction,* River thinks, *I could've found my way to coffee. I'd never feel clean again.*

Most of what the Barclays ship out is fairly old. When the world's collapse began, people purchased whatever they could to hold themselves over. Grocery stores shut their doors permanently when chemicals contaminated farm and water sources, tainting fresh produce and meat. Starving people looted local businesses and homes, amassing huge amounts of processed food – enough to last several years, if not longer.

But many of those people died, victims of thievery and poisoning, their real treasures not jewelry or television sets to be stolen, but cans of unsalted beans. Such was the way.

Supplies ultimately ended up in old warehouses as scavengers formed groups. Most of the compound's supplies come from dingy places like these. It's rumored that there are entire groups who still live out of them, but River has never heard anything to convince her it's the truth. Someday they will run out of stores, but no one will talk about that for now.

Quinn stands solitary at the end of a hall, hunkering down in her usual spot even as the alarms blare. She stares at a wall in boredom, puffing air in and out of her mouth.

"Quinn," River announces, "What are you still doing out here?"

Quinn blows the air out of her mouth, raising her hands as if to say she doesn't have a good answer. "I'm a businesswoman," her raspy voice makes River's skin crawl, "That's what interests me most in this fickle life. What can I do for you?"

"Some bandages. Alcohol. A few rolls of toilet paper and some cocoa, if you have any," River asks, already reaching for her I.D. card. Quinn shrugs her shoulders and takes a little electronic device out of her pocket.

"Alcohol and bandages are fine. Toilet paper I can get you. We haven't had cocoa for a while and it's a waste of currency, if you ask me. Oh, when I do get some, the price is going up,

I'll tell you that. Nobody wants to trade their goodies with me anymore, not with all this drama on people's minds," she responds. She waits while River continues fishing in her pockets. "Lose something, dear?"

"I swear I had it in my back pocket this morning," River croaks.

Quinn nods. "I swear I had a head full of luscious brown hair this morning," she smiles, "But we both know that that just isn't true." She winks.

"I really did lose it. You know I can pay, come on. An IOU?" River begs.

"Oh, you 'lost' it? You and everyone else," she tuts and draws her attention back to the wall as if River is nothing more than a fly buzzing in her face.

River walks away, aghast. Never once has she been unable to pay for something. She sighs and closes her eyes. *If I can't find this damn card, I'm going to have to wipe myself with the pages of classics. Poor Airlee. One roll was for her...*

She huffs her way toward the control room.

It's no wonder Sam selected Quinn to recruit good workers into Rebels; she is, as she said, "all about business." It doesn't matter whose side she really believes in or which individuals she actually likes. The transaction could involve food or shower time or blood – the exact work or compensation doesn't matter. Her allegiance belongs to the highest bidder. It's this that makes River loathe her.

Quinn must have the most shower time of anyone in the compound, yet she still smells like a ripe bucket of sweat, River scrunches her nose.

She stops at her compartment to grab a few hand towels and a bottle of water in lieu of the toilet paper; where Airlee is going, she'll want to be as clean and odor-free as possible.

17 / AIRLEE

*A*irlee senses River's presence in the Detention Center before she sees or hears her. She's back soon, and thank God for that; Airlee's ears can't stop ringing because of the alarms.

"I need to ask a favor of you," River rushes a set of keys out of her pocket and swings open the cell door.

Airlee cups her right hand to her ear. *I can't hear you.* She watches in confusion as River splashes a tattered rag with some water and flinches as she scrubs her down. Black dust coats every thread of the cloth.

"You're going outside! We're losing air," River lifts her gently by the arm and moves her into the hall. "Follow me, we'll walk and talk."

Airlee places her hand around her own neck. *I'll choke.*

"I'm giving you a suit," River huffs, "You'll be safe. The people who come in and out of here wear them and they're doing okay." Despite what she's just learned about the air, the idea of wearing protection still comforts her. At the least, if Airlee manages to come back, she won't suspect the truth.

Airlee's eyes bulge. She points to River, swirls an arm around, brings her hand back to her throat, and motions forward as if the suit was right in front of her. *People have died out there and now you're telling me we have suits?*

River stares in awe at her. She doesn't understand.

"No one knows I'm doing this. Just me and Sam. Promise me you'll come back."

They round a bend. Airlee guesses they're in a far corner of the compound. "You can't feed yourself out there, so escape is pointless," River goes on, "Dying here would be easier if it came down to it, but Sam and I are going to tell everyone you're dead even though you won't be. Maybe I can get in touch with another compound, see if they'll take you in somehow." She thrusts her hand into a closet, determined to move fast before daylight is gone.

Airlee shakes her head, but she's not sure River gets it. *Your promises don't mean anything. I'm going to die a hermit if that's the kind of life you give me.*

On second thought, she reaches her hand out. *Just give me the suit.*

If no one takes care of the problem, she's going to die, anyway. They all will.

"Check the vents. Remove anything blocking them," River says, "Use this brush and liter of water to clean anything that looks clogged. I'm told there's a spigot out there, but I have no idea if it works. Use the water sparingly, and be fast."

Airlee pulls the legs up over her pants and slips her arms through the sleeves. She hesitates at the mask.

River yanks it up over her head without waiting. Heart racing, Airlee can't help but touch her head through the material. It's claustrophobic inside and she can't breathe well through her nose – it's just not how the suit was made to function. Already, she can't wait to take it off, feeling her own hot air warming her. It's obvious now why River washed her up – she can already begin to smell herself in the enclosed space. The task begins to worry her. Can she even pull it off?

Is River too afraid to go out herself? It would explain why she keeps looking down.

"Wait for me to leave to open the door, okay? I don't know what's out there, if there's some kind of decontamination chamber or something. I'll come back here as often as I can. Stay here when you come back in." Airlee nods at her.

An awkward moment passes. It's impossible to make small talk with someone who can't speak, but it's hard to say good-bye, too.

"Well," River says quietly, "Good luck." She tilts her head down, offers a little smile, and backs out of the hallway. Airlee watches her slender hips sway away, the rhythm keeping her from having an anxiety attack. She turns to the hatch and waits for her breath to come back.

If she could laugh at this moment, she would. Of all the ironic things in the world, this moment has to take the cake. And people would still call her a terrorist, never knowing the truth. She only ever wanted what was best for everyone. The people in power would have never listened to a no-one like her.

Now they need her, or face death.

If I wait too long to catch my breath, we're all going to die.

She grips the hatch with both hands and twists hard, committing to the action. As she prepares to step into a new room, a splash of yellow morning light blinds her. She practically falls out of the compound. She uses the giant hands of the suit to block out the sun.

No decontamination chambers. Not even a barrier.

Aware that the door is standing wide open, she leans back on it and seals it shut. *I hope I can get back in okay,* she thinks.

She tilts her head skyward. Puffy clouds cover most of the

expanse, clusters of azure painting an uneven white canvas. Thick trees line the edges of the cracked pavement that surrounds the perimeter of the building.

She peers her head out further to catch a glimpse of the rest of the structure. It's too large to fully see, but most of what is here is covered in brick and thick moss. A few blown-out windows mar the back of the building.

Her feet are moving across the pavement before she has time to process what she's doing. *Time is important here,* she thinks, *do it fast and do it right. Find anything that could be a problem.*

The broken warehouse windows don't faze her in the least. Whoever designed the structure sealed off the underground floors.

Did they, though? There was no decontamination chamber. Weird...

A rustle behind her makes her turn her head. It came from the trees.

She watches for a few seconds, hoping to see a squirrel playing among the branches, but not even a bird chirps. It's unusual for animals to be around the compound; the building's location has always made it vulnerable to winds from the hardest hit places, and once the animals catch that scent, they run. The thing about toxins is that they never just *disappear*;

they're always somewhere, blown by the wind or sucked into the water for the fish to devour and croak on. The ecosystem, last anyone heard, was in pretty strange shape.

Turning back to her task, she follows the pavement around the building, pulling old bird nests and leaves from mysterious pipes and scraping moss off of what she thinks are vents.

She guesses she's about halfway around the building when she feels a slam from underneath her like a bomb going off. The vibration makes its way up her legs, ceasing at her achy knees.

She stops and listens; when the wind doesn't blow, she can hear the faint whine of the alarms firing back up. Whatever happened, there must have been structural damage.

Speaking of structural damage, her next vent is totally destroyed, crushed by an ancient oak. She can hardly see the metal, but she imagines that it's mangled underneath. And there's nothing she can do to fix it.

Something rustles in the distant bushes parallel to her. From about fifty feet away, she sees him; a man covered in green and black camouflage, holding a long gun.

Aiming it at her.

She drops her supplies and sprints forward. The figure takes a shot and the bullet zings off of some metal siding. The front door seems inviting enough, given the circumstances;

she can't keep running or she'll suffocate. She has to hide.

Fortunately, the chains barring entry have been long rusted away. The door crunches open with a hard yank.

She expects her pursuer to taunt her like the easy prey she is, to give his location away in a brief tear of cockiness, but he doesn't. He's smarter than that. *I can't die. People are relying on me. Jesus, I thought no one could live out here! Why is he shooting at me?*

To make matters worse, she can't exactly call out to him to clear up who she is. If that even matters.

He could be a cannibal, she realizes with horror.

The floor, she's surprised to find, doesn't look too rotted out. She creeps across its boards, lurking through the cover of shadows that can't be helping her much – the bulky suit is brighter than a caution sign – but she'll take what cover she can.

There's not much around in the way of weapons – some broken wooden spindles, a curtain rod, a rusty fountain pen. The sharpness of the pen steals her attention. She picks it up.

Halfway through the next room, she sighs through her nose. *I should have picked up the curtain rod. Longer range.* From behind her, she can hear her attacker prowling in the other room. His breaths come heavy and ventilated. *He's too close,* she thinks.

With no other rooms to travel through, she's stuck. He's going to find her. She sinks behind a desk in the corner and prays for the best. There is no plan.

The man's footsteps circle the room as he searches its every inch. Airlee fights the urge to peek her head up to get a look at him; the last thing she needs is to get her head blown off. She slowly backs further into the corner. Her pinky finger brushes up against something hard on the floor.

She picks the object up gingerly. The corners of her eyes turn up as she feels its weight. It's some kind of glass ball, forged before the War began. All these years collecting dirt in the warehouse, and it's made its way into her hands to be shattered for this purpose. She has no idea who this man is, but she's determined to end him before he ends her.

In a leap of faith, she chucks the glass orb against a window ten feet diagonal to her. There's not much time to react. She can't think about what happens next.

Airlee launches herself over the desk and into the man as he reacts to the sound. She barely processes his ghastly black gas mask before she jams the pen into the side of his neck and rapidly twists it. A single spurt of blood spits out. The pen doesn't seem like the worst choice of weapon anymore.

The man screams in agony. He collects her from behind in one swoop and thrusts his body backwards into the cracked window, sending hers crashing two stories below.

Bang, bang! He shoots out from the dangling shards of glass. Just for good measure.

18 / RIVER

"You opened that door a lot faster than I expected," River says, mostly to herself. Sweat beads her forehead. If they all survive this crisis, Milan's name will become legendary. His feat will probably be overshadowed by what's to come, but there's not much anyone can do about that.

She can taste the tension in the control room.

"And I could've opened it faster, too," Milan retorts, grimacing at Samuel.

"Well, the most important thing is that it got done," Samuel says. Milan raises an eyebrow and stands, then brushes off his knees.

The crowd standing by the doorway disperses like flies as soon as they hear the news. A few stragglers hover around the area, not sure if they should stay or go. Most people rush in different directions, many jogging towards the main hatch to watch it open. Some head to less frequently used doors.

Guards and nurses burst in through the main hatch, the stench of fear flowing outward. Shouts of "close the door!" pour from the mouths of the first to fly through. The little foyer hardly holds the mass assembly of people there originally – let alone the escapees. They push back the crowd until people begin cracking into each other's ribs, some falling on the ground and being plodded over.

The first thing River notices after the initial wave of incomers is the noise – men and women screaming, objects banging around, grunting. Anxiety overflows in her as she realizes the hysteria isn't over. She rushes over to the security room – oxygen levels dropped about a half percent while she was gone, but have stabilized somewhere in the last twenty minutes.

"What happened?" Samuel hollers, addressing anyone and everyone. No one even acknowledges him. Their prime objective is to reach a safe haven.

Unfortunately, those at the back of the group are too late. Men with red bandanas tote lead pipes in the distance. They thwack them against the walls, against bodies wriggling on the floor.

"Shut the doors!" Samuel shouts to the guards posted by the hatch, tearing at his hair with both hands. The men stop ushering people in for a moment, but stare dumbfounded as hordes continue to ram through; if it comes down to it, they know what will happen. Their own people will turn on them. The guards nod at each other in a gesture of comradery – if they have to explain themselves later, they will say that they didn't hear Samuel. It's believable enough.

River beholds the tumult with sadness and awe. Not only do guards and nurses surge through the hatch into the Most Privileged side, but workers, as well – people seek shelter in their enemies' arms. River recognizes a few kids from the cages; their cells must have opened automatically when Milan unlocked the doors. For some of them, it's their first time moving significantly in years.

The guards appear more beat up as the end of the herd draws near. A handful of people limp through the hatch at a time. A few shake their heads, signaling that the struggle is over. One of the men standing by the door shuts it tight, locking out a dozen or more stragglers as the perpetrators close in.

"Now will someone tell me what is going on?" Samuel bellows.

"They attacked the greenhouse," a nurse says, covering her black eye with one bloody hand.

"They destroyed everything. There's no fresh food *left*," the guard next to her cries. Oddly enough, he's in better shape than she is. Samuel feels a pang of guilt as he wonders if she fought harder than the guard. He never could understand why year after year, the Council stuck to its gender roles.

"Without us, they won't get fed. It's suicide!" a nurse at the front of the crowd yells.

"Nobody impresses on them the things we do to help them," a graying man steps out of the crowd and addresses Samuel, "Nobody thinks they're worth the time to be included in the conversation about the compound, even after all this. We keep treating them like workhorses to feed the War! The majority of them *believe* we need each other even if they don't understand why, but the 10% who are angry enough to take action *will* ruin things for everyone. They already have. Please, Sam. Tell the Council how it really is!"

"Nobody asked you for your opinion. If you don't shut yourself up, I might do it for you," Meyer spits. He fingers the worn fibers of his belt and steadies his eyes against the wall.

"No, but I did live there with my wife for most of my life. We raised an orphan girl until we grew old and our hands couldn't do the work they were meant to do. We transitioned to this community late, but I know those people well," the man says, "Probably better than you do, young man. And frankly, if you don't believe that some of your own men were out there axing people away, you're more out of touch than I thought."

"Can it, Murphy," Meyer smirks, "Your orphan girl is set to

be executed. What does that say about you?"

* * *

River changes into an old silk nightgown before heading to bed. She's checked the hallway for Airlee several times now and so far, no luck. By now, only the worst could have happened. Her heart sits heavy in her chest.

She only faintly hears Samuel moving around in bed across the room; the noise of the day has left an obnoxious ringing in her ears and an empty numbness in her body, all the adrenaline having ravaged her nerves.

She stares into the bedroom mirror, letting her mind go until she is neither in this world or another. In her crimson red gown, she feels like another person, like the whole situation could just be a bad dream. But she knows it isn't. It's real.

Without meaning to, River has killed someone.

"Are you okay?" Samuel asks in a gentle voice. He reaches out and strokes her small triceps. The warmth of his skin against her cold body shocks her back to life. She shakes her head.

"I'm fine," she says, "Just meditating, I guess."

"I think we could all do a little meditating," Samuel laughs sarcastically and plops himself back on the hard bed. He rubs his eyes with both hands – a bad habit brought on by stress. During these times, he looks so childish. Usually River can't help but find something adorable about him expressing his vulnerable side, but she's worried now, too. The compound could collapse. He knows by her silence that she's affected, too.

She walks over to the bed and sits by him without touching him. She longs to support him, to lie and tell him that she knows everything will be okay – life always finds a way – but discovers that she's experienced too many sensations for one day. Every last drop of her energy has been sapped. She can't even bring herself to reach out and stroke his hair. She silently watches him as he begins rubbing his temples. Next, she knows, he'll rub his jaw; never even realizing that the reason it hurts is because he's been clenching his teeth.

"Did you see anyone specific missing?" Samuel asks.

River chews on the question for a moment. Absolutely, people had been left behind. Who they might be, she isn't sure. There are a few faces she doesn't recall seeing, but everyone rushed in so fast. The question almost seems like a trick at first, as if Samuel is really asking, "Who do you care about enough to look for?"

Comparing notes seems sensible. They had both been too tired to officially track losses.

"I didn't see Edwin," River says. "Do you think he came back?"

Samuel sighs. "Being how he is now, it wouldn't surprise me if someone took him hostage."

"If that's the case, we'll get him back."

"I sure hope so," Samuel replies, "We invested so much in him."

Samuel sits up, positioning himself so that he lies next to her. She covers herself up with their worn blankets and he follows her lead, settling into the uncomfortable mattress they've shared for years. He shifts to his side and places one hand on her small stomach. She shivers at the feel of his fingers gently stroking her, but frowns.

"What's wrong?"

River stays quiet, staring into the abyss of the dark room. After a moment, she speaks.

"What isn't wrong?"

"The way things have been going, it's easy to think that. We have each other, though. For now, we have our health. We're very fortunate to be here, where it's safe. Things will get better. They always do."

"How do you know that things are safe? This could be our last night together. What if they take me and threaten to kill me if you don't do what they say? I don't want you to be their slave forever," she says, "And here, things with the Rebellion have gotten so much more violent than I ever expected. Nothing has ever been this bad." She glances over at him from her pillow, tears spilling over. She wipes them away with the back of her hand.

Sam remains quiet for a moment. "I don't know for sure, but I have a feeling things will be okay somehow. We'll all go on living, remembering this as if it were some cosmic joke."

"Someone asked yesterday why we don't have kids even though we're on the list," River states. She hears Sam's pillow ruffle as he readjusts himself.

"Someday we'll wind up with them, whether we want them or not. Just like in the old days."

"I only have so long. They'll move on and add someone else to the list."

River stares at the ceiling, frozen like a statue. What kind of conversation was this after a day like today? Twenty-four hours, each one conspiring against her.

"I don't think I want children in a world like this," River whispers, her voice muddled by briny tears. Aside from the obvious stress of raising a child in a war zone, she can't imagine being personally responsible for a life 24 hours a day; feeding, changing, showing love and tenderness when there's absolutely no energy for it. Tending to her own needs has become a problem, never mind looking over an infant. She detaches some hair stuck to her lips and exhales, waiting for his response.

The geneticists proclaimed that she and Samuel would be an excellent match, but the fact remains that *better* biological matches for River exist. Samuel's thoughts regarding who should be the biological father, River knows, will stem from his loyalty to the compound rather than to her. In the end, they would raise a complete stranger's child, never knowing what the combination of their love for each other could produce.

"I don't either," his nostrils flare up – a dead giveaway that his eyes are watering.

"Things were different the last time we talked about it," River explains even though she doesn't need to.

"Yes. They were," Samuel laughs weakly, his voice already waterlogged. He's never said out loud before that he doesn't think kids are a good idea.

"We're the reason that dumb people took over the world, you know," River presses her hand against his arm, "People like us."

She picks at her cuticles; a bad habit formed when she first began nurses' training. Anxiety, she was told, had some fairly decent treatments in the old days. Now, finding so little as an ibuprofen is a blessing. She decides to change the subject.

"We're supposed to have a symbiotic relationship with the

workers, but from the day we started altering them, it never really was that way. We've always been using them," River releases it all in one breath, "Same way the Barclays are using us."

"There's a reason we targeted Airlee, you know – to find a reason to let her go. She was smart and angry, and that's a deadly combination."

"So, we killed her," River says, her voice monotone. He doesn't disagree.

"We can use her as an example to others. That's exactly what we need right now. People need to learn that they can't keep getting away with this crap. Letting her go is the merciful thing to do. If we don't, people could keep getting hurt."

"People would get hurt no matter which way we chose. No one even gave Airlee the opportunity to explain herself," River starts, but Sam cuts her off.

"What is there to explain, River? We found a map going through escape routes. Quinn must have had a good laugh, pretending to know the ins and outs of the compound, but she came pretty close to one of the exits. Imagine a scenario in which she escapes and leads the others out. Do you understand how bad that would be? Not just for us, but for the country? Maybe humanity? There aren't many of us left anymore. Hundreds of millions at most."

"Oh, for all you know, China's still home to a billion people and *we* were the only ones wiped off the map," River sighs, "According to you, the air is clean now, but we can't go outside, which I don't understand. None of us has heard from the military. It's like they don't even exi-"

River's jaw swings open and she stops in her tracks. After all this time, the reality was so horribly easy.

"I'd bet everything I own that our ancestors suffered the way we have. Same story, different plot. The First Worlds brought their misery to every country on Earth with their cars and planes, knowing the wrongs they committed but doing them, anyway. It's fitting that our military was one that failed."

Their eyes meet in the darkness. Years of lies and the truth finally comes out.

"Alder might not live much longer. If anything happens to us, no one will know the truth of who we really are; who we've always been. The Barclays, on the other hand, aren't real."

Sam pulls a chain out from under his shirt. On its end is an old silver key. He loops the chain around his neck and fits the key into the middle drawer of his nightstand. River always thought the key was symbolic, a fashion statement. Now, she realizes, it's always had a purpose.

"You can't be saying that we've been slaves for generations," River says, "giving things to someone other than our military."

He hands a small notebook out to her.

"That's exactly what I'm saying, River. We lost the War," he chews his lip nervously in the dark, "Read this tomorrow while you're hiding. You'll learn everything you need to know."

Her neck tenses up. "If it isn't the Barclays coming tomorrow, then who is it?"

19 / AIRLEE

$\mathcal{E}$verything around her is bathed in shades of blue, the black tops of the trees swaying in quick bursts of wind. Stars twinkle above, the great expanse of the Milky Way showing itself off. The woods her body has been moved to are filled with sounds, but she can't identify a single one of them.

Airlee cranes her head to the left and then to the right, struggling to investigate her surroundings. There's no evidence the man in the mask is still hanging around. He must have thought she was dead and dumped her body.

She can't tell if he dragged her to this spot or if the pain is 100% from the fall. Two of her fingers are certainly broken. A sharp spasm travels through her back every time she moves, and her neck and ankles feel sprained. Fortunately, the thick grass broke her fall, but she still feels like a train wreck. The second story window she fell out of wasn't very high, but high enough. She tries to prop herself up with her elbows, but the pain in her back drives her to the ground.

The sky grows darker with every minute that passes, the yellow horizon shrinking and giving way to the light of the full moon. *Funny,* Airlee thinks, *I may be the only person from the compound who's ever seen the stars like this.*

A rustle in the bushes grabs her attention. She closes her eyes again and plays dead just in case the man has returned. She feels movement around her body and the sound of heavy breathing.

Something touches Airlee's hand, something wet. She tries not to react, but when she feels the unfamiliar touch of fur nuzzling her, her eyes bolt open. Standing next to her with a look of curiosity is a wolf pup, its mother surely not too far off.

Airlee fights through the pain and lifts herself off the ground. She doesn't want to be around when the animal's mother comes around. Not until she's standing does she realize what's happened to her suit.

The arms hang in thick shreds; proof enough that her attacker dragged her here. The breeze in the back of the suit suggests the same, but she doesn't have the strength to confirm. Her mask is cracked, but not completely shattered; not that it matters with the rest of the equipment in tatters. Somehow the legs of the suit are still intact, save for a half-moon hole in the side of her left leg. She pokes at it and winces. She can't remember anything after hitting the ground, but he must have grazed her with a bullet.

How could he have missed me from so close? Lucky for me he couldn't handle his gun, she thinks.

Other questions plague her, as well. How is she not dead? Isn't the air toxic? Animals are supposed to fear humans, so why has one just approached her?

Gunfire erupts in the distance, each shot measured and deliberate. The shooter is aiming at something. *Time to go.*

The little wolf follows her all the way to the edge of the woods, where its high-pitched howl echoes throughout the clearing. Airlee contemplates taking him with her, proving that Sam has been lying all along.

The compound is in her sights, a ten-minute walk away. Under the cover of darkness, she knows she can bridge the gap.

Airlee hears gunfire from inside the woods - she doesn't have time to turn her head before the bullet grazes her right arm. Knowing she'd make an easy target in the clearing, she bounds back into the woods away from the sound of the weapon, every step sending fire up and down her spine. Her attacker isn't very far away.

The shreds of her sleeves keep getting caught on branches, slowing her down. Before she knows it, he's right behind her, the only thing separating them a line of thick trees.

In the darkness, she doesn't see the small pond before she steps into it. Its water ripples before her, but it's too late to turn back. She keeps moving, her even movements generating no noise. As the water submerges her upper body, she places her hands around her neck and grips as hard as she can with her broken fingers, creating a seal between her cracked helmet and the water. With any luck, it will hold.

His footsteps are barely audible, but loud enough to hear him around the edge of the pond. He must be familiar with these woods; he completely skirts the water. A rustle in some bushes makes him rush away deeper into the trees. Airlee waits a minute for him to create some distance and peels herself out of the pond. Waiting for her at the water's edge is the wolf pup. It offers her a happy wag and nudges its head at her injured leg.

Airlee's eyes crinkle in a smile; the little creature saved her by creating a distraction. Maybe it was coincidence. Maybe it wasn't the wolf at all. She knows what she prefers to think.

She ducks behind some trees and takes a look at herself. The suit is too vibrant; she'll have to take it off to make it back to the compound safely. She unseals the mask, shrugs off the ragged material, and stuffs everything between a bush and a tree. Her jumper should be dark enough to allow her some cover.

In her rush, she doesn't have time to savor her first real breath of fresh air. It's sweeter than she ever imagined, a sort of cherry medicine scent hanging in the atmosphere.

The wolf pup follows her again to the edge of the woods. The yellow band on the horizon has faded, a medium blue taking its place. Airlee thinks she sees the compound in the distance, but can't be certain now. Things have gotten significantly darker in a short period of time.

The little pup scampers forward over to a large bulge in the terrain and whines. He nudges the bulge in quick, anxious movements. She steps toward the creature to see what the mass is. Shot right between the eyes is the pup's mother, its killer spelling out death for her vulnerable kin.

If Airlee has to guess based on how the body was abandoned, the shooter doesn't care about the meat at all. He's shooting for the fun of it.

* * *

Airlee arrives at the compound twenty minutes later. The distance had grown a little since her last attempt, and the darkness didn't help her any. She strokes the furry, grey bundle in her arms. He nuzzles her neck, terrified; his legs quake against her arms.

It takes her a few minutes to find the same door she originally exited, but when she does, she realizes in awe that there really is no way back in through the door. She tries a few others to the same effect. Finally, she heads back to the original door and wails on it, praying that someone inside hears it before the man in the mask does. She has nowhere else to go but back into the wilderness.

The creaky hatch begins turning from the inside of the compound. In under ten seconds, the door swings open. She rushes past the hesitant face behind it and slams it shut.

"What are *you* doing here?" Sanguine asks, his eyes taking in one hell of a mess. Water pools at Airlee's feet. The pup growls from under her protective hold.

"Is that a dog?" he asks, about to step closer in amazement. He stops himself. "What if he's sick? How are you even alive?"

Airlee stares at him, too worn out to try to explain. Sanguine pulls a red handkerchief from his pocket and hands it to her. "Your mask came off," he tells her. The adrenaline coursing through her veins must have blocked that embarrassing fact out.

She accepts it gingerly. There's something murderous about the man, but soft, as well. Unknown to her, he's already put it all together. His theory about the compound, he now knows, has always been correct.

"Follow me. I'll get you someplace safe," he places the palm of his hand on her wet back and leads her forward, down through a locked room leading to a hidden hallway filled with empty rooms. When he leaves, he doesn't lock the barred door behind him, allowing her to come and go as she pleases.

20 / EDWIN

*W*ork has quickly become ordinary to me, the relentless cycles of emotion washing over my body and leaving nothing in their wake. I doubt that anything I'll experience will compare to last night, though.

As my shift in the carpentry shop was about to end, a monster explosion rocked the compound. The sound came from deep within – the greenhouse, I later learned. The workers looked up from their little paintbrushes with limited interest. I forced myself to the door, expecting the noise to have been a simple clap of thunder, my imagination exaggerating the sound. I peeked my head into the empty hallway, hoping.

Panicked screams erupted from Luna Bay, prompting other guards to stick their heads out of doors. Nurses and workers fled in our direction, some covered in blood, most without any apparent injuries. I merely watched as the first few sped past, trailing crimson on the floor. They disappeared around a corner, leaving distant tearful sobs and cries of warning behind them.

I clutched my baton, prepared for anything, but as the Rebels approached, I froze; internally, I wanted to barricade myself in the shop, but couldn't make my legs move. Aside from the harsh clang of their metallic weapons and the footsteps of old, heavy work boots, they kept silent. Most of them wore red bandanas, exposing only their angry eyes.

One of the Rebels stuck out to me; his pace didn't change, but it was all the motivation I needed to back out of the hallway, slam the door shut, and push over a half empty filing cabinet to block entry.

"Help me with these tables!" I yelled to no one in particular before turning around. Several workers were already on their feet behind me, ready to pitch in. They piled whatever they could in front of the door; tables, chairs, heavy paint cans. Their cooperation stunned me, but looking back, I suppose it shouldn't have; most of these workers had recently been promoted. They wanted – needed – to prove their worth. I remember that feeling well.

One of the workers tapped me on the shoulder, seeking more direction. I just watched as the group of Rebels passed by, the closest member staring in at me through a small window in the door. He continued watching me, his eyebrows furrowing as if deciding if he should break in and end me. With an ominous slam of his fist on the wood, he spun away and rejoined his friends. Behind them they dragged a severed leg, their message of dominance perfectly transparent. The doors visible from my point of view were wide open – I figured the thugs wanted guards only, but no. We watched together in horror as a glass worker was dragged into the hallway and stomped to death, each cracked rib making us collectively wince. Marty, I believe his name was – known for ratting out other workers for their mistakes. This was how he hoped to thrive.

He never got promoted, and he didn't survive. The ultimate failure.

The workers behind me started choking on their own tears, slowly suffocating as they hyperventilated through their noses. Whoever this band of Rebels was, they wanted us to watch. *All of us.*

For agonizing hours, we remained stuck in the shop like rabbits in a fox den. The stink of anxious sweat filled the room and the men took to urinating in empty paint cans, patience wearing thin. A distance down the hall, people banged on the hatch, begging for entry into the other side of the compound. The explosion locked the main doors – a good thing, as most guards were with the workers to protect them.

However, even we couldn't contain the disaster well. The Most Privileged would never be able to handle these killers on their own.

I was far from the only one cowering, but a few braved the horde. Other guards growled as they struggled with the Rebels, the sounds of fighting giving way to silence. More footsteps. Finally, the attackers retreated to the back of the compound, I assume to Luna Bay. Their numbers seemed as steady as when they'd first walked past my door, but maybe it was my imagination.

A wave of people pushed through the hatch to the other side of the compound as soon as the door unlocked. I was too afraid to head in that direction; confronting the sight of blood everywhere was not on my immediate to-do list. My teeth chattered from the pure adrenaline rush. I had to do something, but I couldn't decide what. On an impulse, I ripped the furniture away from the rickety door, the workers only watching in awe this time.

I tore open the door and waved at everyone to follow me, but chaos ensued. My workers escaped into various hallways, many of which don't have exits. I ran down a small hallway little used and often forgotten, having completely failed to keep anyone by my side. At the end of the hall was a high staircase leading to another entrance to the other side of the compound.

"Go, go, get out of here!" a familiar voice called from behind me. I whipped around and watched his dirty hands as he shooed me onto the staircase, backing my body through the doorway.

It was Sanguine, his red handkerchief wrapped securely around his face.

"You look like one of dem," I said, my hands involuntarily balling up into fists behind my back and out of his sight.

"I knew this would be violent, but not like this," he said. All the heat in my body rose to my face.

"You bastard. How many are hurt?" I got in his face, not quite sure how threatening I sounded, but still trying.

"More workers than guards. I saw people swinging weapons at random. It wasn't supposed to be a bloodbath," he answered. The way his eyes darted around made me certain he had something to feel guilty about.

"Why did you do it? So many people were at risk of getting hurt!" I looked him solidly in the eyes and waited for a response.

"You know the truth of this place – the mutilations, the way everyone stays in line. For what? Our lives cannot amount to guarding starving people who make tables and chairs for some rich snobs. I'm living a false life, Edwin, and so are you, thinking that we're better than where we came from. We have to strive for something greater for *everyone*, even if it's just for the right to be born intact or choose death by walking outdoors. I'd give anything to feel the sunshine on my face. Wouldn't you?"

Fire burned my cheeks. I wanted so furiously to cast him aside, beat him, report him to higher authorities and blame him for all the casualties, but I found myself hesitantly agreeing. What about all the harm done to people quietly over the years? We *should* be able to choose our deaths. We *should* be born healthy and whole and not have to face mutilation as punishment for poor behavior. Isn't poor behavior subjective, anyway?

Of course, though, I didn't lay a finger on him. It's not in my nature.

"At least you're telling me da truth," I croaked.

Sanguine's eyes widened. He wasn't expecting a tame response.

It dawned on me that our actions may be different, but our dreams were not. We both had higher hopes for the compound. I kept my wishes secret and viewed them as impossibilities; his wishes were in the open, ripe and *desired* enough to prompt action, however poorly thought out. Under different circumstances, he could have swayed me to join the Rebellion.

Was Airlee a part of the most violent subgroups? I can't imagine it, but there's no way of knowing.

My lips went taut. "Jus' follow me," I instructed. I ascended the stairs, Sanguine acting as my shadow. Not a drop of blood sullied his clothes. With that in mind, I decided to keep quiet for a while, figuring he might have been a good person who got in over his head. If I told anyone, he would surely die.

At the top of the stairs, I turned and looked him in the eye for what felt like an eternity, sending a silent message. *We have an agreement. No more bloodshed.*

He nodded.

* * *

Since the attack, I've avoided contact with anyone. I can't bear to look at another human being.

Everyone has been ordered not to return to work for the time being. The hatch and all other exits to the other side have been sealed off; none of the workers abandoned there are being fed. Nurses tend to the victims on our side of the compound with little rest. They're expected to visit the other side later today or early tomorrow, long after those with the worst injuries will have perished. Several guards have volunteered to go back over, but Meyer has swiftly denied their requests.

No one has even mentioned catching the attackers. At this scale, it's like no one believes it can be done.

After spending the night sweating in fear and fury, thinking about the blood-soaked floors, I feel dirty. With nothing else to do and no first aid skills, it seems that the best place for me is in a shower. I need to clear my mind. The water isn't warm, the soap is crudely made and leaves slippery scum behind, but there's no place I'd rather be. If only water could wash away guilt.

The eerie quiet of the hallways raises the hairs on my neck. Most of the action is in the lobby, where a quick walk-through reveals wounds varying from gashes to burns and amputations. Already, nurses seem to be run ragged. Most of them appear on the verge of tears. They've been sleeping in shifts, but if they've been sleeping the way I did, they might as well be working drunk.

"Edwin," the check-in guard, Joe, says, "We don't see you in the showers much lately." He offers me a forced smile.

I suppose I stink. Great.

"I thought no one was supposed to work?"

"No one is supposed to be working *over there*. No one *has to* work over here. If anyone asks, I'm not working. I'm *socializing*." He smirks. Joe is not known for his sociability.

"Thanks, Joe, but I'm jus' here for a shower," I say, fidgeting with the loose strings on the end of my sleeve.

"Of course you are," he says, "Nobody comes just to talk to

Old Joe. We'll need your identification card, then." He eyes my pockets and motions with his hand for me to give it to him.

I reach into my back pocket, expecting to find it on my right side. It's not there. Nervousness pours into my bones, filling my body with electric anxiety. *This is the pocket I always keep it in.* I check the other back pocket and the front ones, as well. Nothing.

"No card, no shower, my friend," Joe shakes his head impatiently.

"I jus' had it. Is there any way you can make a note? Say I owe points, at least 'til I find it?" I ask. I'm beginning to find that I articulate best when nervous. I've had a lot of experience with that lately.

How could I have lost it? Did it somehow slip out of my pocket during all of the commotion in the carpentry shop? Running down the halls? Climbing the stairs?

Definitely not. I'd felt its stiffness against me while I moved around. When was the last time I had it?

"Ha!" he bellows. "If I could make notes *or something,* there wouldn't be a need for the damned card, would there be?"

I think the last place I'd had it was at the top of the stairs with Sanguine...

"If you can't find it, make a trade. I'm sure you have something useful," Joe's words drip with sarcasm.

Sanguine. He snatched it out of my back pocket after we climbed the stairs. *While I helped him escape.*

"Someone stole it," I say frantically.

"Well, then, you should guard your property more carefully, shouldn't you? You are a guard, after all. That's your job. If you can't guard a little card properly..." He trails off, laughing, trying to get a rise out of me. I guess the events of the past day aren't enough for him to chew on.

"Joe, if you're just here 'socializing,' I can do whatever the hell I want to."

He's struck speechless for a couple of seconds. "You can't say that to *me*, I've been doing this for twenty-five damn years!"

"If you wanna tell the Council you disobeyed them, go ahead," I wink at him as I breeze by, feeling power surge through my body as he begrudgingly lets me through.

For the first time in my life, I've taken power. The toxic elixir flows through my veins. I disrobe in a dream.

I smirk involuntarily as the water washes over me, purifying my body and soul – at least temporarily.

I pat myself dry with a fresh community towel and revel in my first shower in days. I'm not sure how I ever lived a life bereft of cleanliness. My skin tingles, finally able to breathe.

I wink at Joe again on the way out of the shower room. He crosses his arms and shakes his head. The smile stays with me as I walk the halls, my confidence restored.

Sanguine, Sanguine. I will find you, and take back what's mine.

21 / AIRLEE

*I*f you look at a ceiling long enough, shapes emerge from the cracks, stains, and other imperfections. This is what Airlee has found for entertainment in the hallway, staring until her eyes grow tired and one shape morphs its way into another. One moment a giraffe, the next a lopsided candy cane. *I'm going insane,* she thinks.

For hours late last night, the alarms had been going off. They occupied her for a while; she banged on the bars of the door for someone to come to her attention, but no one came. No one heard her from deep in the basement. *What if there's an emergency and they forget me?* she thought. *What if I die in here of smoke inhalation or some other terrible thing?*

Sanguine had left her free to roam; she could have gone outside, not that it would be her first choice. He told his boss about what happened, though, and she locked her in.

At first, she felt helpless; then as time passed, she only felt annoyed. It took her a moment to process when the alarms stopped.

Now, after all the excitement of the last twenty-four hours, her imagination fails her; the only thing at the forefront of her mind is the ringing in her ears. She can't even zone out long enough to imagine a pair of eyes on the ceiling, one of the easiest shapes to see. *Everybody likes to imagine some part of themselves in something else, I guess.*

She remembers reading about vehicles in psychology magazines, and about how many were designed specifically to look like a face - appeal to people's desire for connection with other humans. So many things are shaped like faces – vehicles, windows, electrical outlets. The phenomenon is called pareidolia, and usually it's unintentional.

If they don't get me out soon, I'm going to become best friends with my long-nosed sink faucet.

Despite her field trip and the pain she's in, she's antsy already. She's can't imagine living her whole life like this, locked up alone in a stuffy, characterless prison. As she contemplates whether or not she would want to die in the event of actually losing her mind, a door opens. Airlee doesn't bother to see who it is.

"If you can still hear, raise a hand," River smiles gently.

Airlee raises her left wrist off the floor in a limp attempt at complying. Although the company is welcome, numbness is, moreso. The isolation and trauma have broken her down.

River tosses a notebook next to Airlee's hand. A pencil follows, bouncing hard against the wall and rolling back toward the notebook.

"Sorry. You might want to check if I broke that," River says, "We have a lot to talk about."

Airlee reluctantly sits up, waits for the room to stop spinning, and then stands. She holds onto the bars of the door for support as she gets a second head rush.

"Ah, that should be topic number one," River says, "Our oxygen levels are still low. That's why the alarms are still going off every now and then."

Airlee's blood boils. Did she risk her life for nothing? She scribbles on the paper. *Why's that?*

"The Rebels damaged our main air filter during the initial attack. There are people working on it. You did an excellent job helping – thank you – but to survive, we're going to have to focus on the Rebels," she says, her eyes glittering with sadness.

Why are you really here?

"Sam told me something. I haven't told anyone else," she looks down, "I figure I owe this to you."

River bends over and whispers into her ear, explaining

everything Samuel told her – that they'd lost the War decades ago, that generations of Council leaders lied to protect everyone from rebelling and getting themselves killed. They'd kept the community together all these years while everyone insisted the Council was the reason it was falling apart. But now, the men who really rule are coming, and there's nothing they can do but hide.

Panic rises in Airlee's throat. *Where am I?* she jots down. She looks past the bars as she slips the notebook through.

"The basement," River states. "You're safe from them here. They're revolted by us, so they won't go very far."

Airlee tries to think of other questions she'd like to ask while she can.

Do you know anything about what happened to Murphy and Alise?

River keeps her head down for a moment, reading the words repeatedly. She's surprised Airlee doesn't care more about the fact that they're all prisoners, lied to for years. Her focus is still on the compound, the day-to-day injustice. River looks up, looks back down again, and sighs.

"You thought we killed them because they were old, didn't you?"

Airlee nods her head solemnly. *No matter what's happening out there, we still need to deal with each other in here.*

"It's true that it's happened before. People get old, they get sick. They can't pull their weight and they become a burden on resources," she says, gently lowering her voice, "But it *is* done out of mercy. Imagine living in a world where you can't speak, you can barely breathe, and everything hurts, but you can't really communicate *how*. We don't have the medicine to take care of the pain and we can't correct everyone's disfigurements. Alise and Murphy were special, though. It's been a long while since we permitted them to work on my side of the compound, but they're still there. In their prime, they did basic engineering. They've since moved on to different things. Both are very bright."

Airlee gawks at her.

Why did no one tell me about this?

"We don't like our people crossing lines if they don't have to. It's upsetting for everyone. It's one of the reasons guards don't chat with the Least Privileged. It's harder for them that way."

Airlee wrings her clammy hands and adjusts her line of vision. She's not used to conversing in this way – most of her communication has been nonverbal or one-way. Writing is slow and brings out her lack of patience.

Can I see them?

"I don't want to make you promises I can't keep. I may

have already made a few and I'd hate to disappoint you more than I already might."

Airlee doesn't quite know what to ask beyond this point – perhaps the obvious questions, like how they are and if they've ever pushed for a visit. Has she messed up her chances of ever seeing them again? She thumps back down onto the floor next to the bars and sticks the notebook and pencil out.

River purses her lips and looks down on Airlee. "I'll be back to look at your wounds," she whispers, "I won't be more than ten minutes."

She turns briskly on her feet and heads for the exit, hoping to make it to the nurse's station before the raid begins. The sooner she tends to Airlee's wounds, the less likely it'll be that they'll get infected.

Airlee leans her head against the cold iron bars and rubs the dust off of them with her left index finger. Her last creation on this Earth would not be a beautifully crafted toy or piece of furniture, but a blotchy blob on some metal doomed to be filled in, erasing any trace of her presence. Nothing exists for anyone to remember her by. *Such is life,* she thinks, *you die the same way you live.*

Airlee can see into a few other rooms down the hall from where she lays. The hallway appears to end at first glance, but really extends to the left and right; she hadn't paid attention to the shadows there before, but the faded cream-colored walls are not quite the same shade. Even though she's trapped, knowing that a little lies beyond her vision relieves some of her claustrophobia. She strains her neck to see further, but fails to see anything new other than an ugly scuff mark on the wall.

She snorts from her nose and lies on her back, concentrating on making shapes in the ceiling again. The legs of an elephant emerge, but disappear just as fast – as do a flower and a stop sign. She crosses her arms over her stomach, hoping to preserve some warmth.

She considers shutting her eyes and taking yet another long nap, but now she's too wired. If any truth lies in River's words, it could be life changing. If they're true, everyone in the compound is just slaves.

How many people does she know who've died from exhaustion alone?

An orange shape flutters around the wall, hugging the ceiling. Airlee blinks hard, sure something is wrong with her vision. The shape hovers closer, its wings becoming more pronounced. Her eyes follow it all the way down the hall, where it comes to rest gracefully on the ceiling – just above her waist.

It's an orange butterfly, its wings rimmed with black and speckled with white. It fans its body out as Airlee watches with keen interest.

It's a monarch butterfly; Airlee had read about them once, what seems like ages ago. The majestic little creatures became endangered before the War, yet here one is despite all odds, flapping its finely shaped wings like no better place exists on Earth. How could such a small insect carry so much magic in its beauty? She soaks in every detail of the experience, trying to memorize every marking from its bright color to what seems like a pair of tiny eyes embedded on its wings.

The wolf pup scampers to her down the hallway. Fortunately, River let her keep him after Airlee explained the story about its mother. He stops and licks her face. She scratches his soft, dirty belly and he plops down next to her head, breathing gently on her face.

There's hope. Maybe not for her, maybe not for anyone in the compound, but for humanity in general. As long as they live, they have a chance to get it right.

Airlee fingers the open wounds on her arm and leg, wondering what the hell is taking River so long.

22 / EDWIN

Scouring the halls for Sanguine is all Edwin can do to keep himself occupied. By now, nurses have started crossing over, but only the most experienced guards have been granted access to the deepest parts of the Least Privileged quarters. Word is that there are very few additional survivors; what a horrible story the medical officer will have for the Barclays when he heads home.

Edwin is in the lobby people watching when Samuel's voice clicks into life on the intercom:

"Attention residents," he slurs, "We lost twenty souls in the events of the last day; twenty hardworking individuals with hopes and dreams just like yours and mine. Everyone, there is a cancer in this community and if we don't work together in fighting it, we will all go down. In the aftermath of the biggest coordinated attack this compound has ever seen, during a war in which our country could cease to exist, I simply don't know what to say. Let us pray for those we've lost, both in body and in mind."

A moment's pause fills the lobby. Edwin becomes acutely aware that some of the bodies on the floor aren't just resting; some have been abandoned in death. He wonders if they've been included in the casualty count.

"It is with dismay that I announce the death of one of our inmates, known as Airlee. Although we normally don't announce executions, we feel it's necessary. Airlee was a member of the Rebellion, the group responsible for these heinous crimes. The attack, we've learned, was orchestrated in order to avenge her arrest. Let this be clear: if you are caught as a member of the Rebellion, you, too, will suffer the same fate. This shortsighted fever will no longer be humored. If anyone has any information about the attack or about the Rebellion, please come forward. Thank you."

Most people continue on with their activities as though the report is nothing more than a quick flash on their radars.

Not Edwin, though. He turns his face to the wall and lets the sting of tears reach his eyes. Airlee, dead. Nearly two-dozen others lifeless. He hangs his head and sobs quietly.

It takes him a few minutes to pull himself together. He barely knew her.

But he wanted to.

He paces the lobby thoughtlessly, watching a mess of people of all Privileges working together to clean and patch each other up. A flurry of sign language takes over the corridor, but the Most Privileged don't understand it. Edwin turns away from it all – too many sensations in one place. They're wracking his nerves.

He spots Meyer down the hall, surveying the damage. Edwin raises his hand to get his attention. Meyer nods his head and picks up his pace just slightly.

"Is it true?" Edwin asks.

Meyer's mind is in a fog; he'd barely heard Samuel's announcement. He was too deep in his own head.

"Is what true?" Meyer asks, his sandpapery voice extra hoarse.

"Is Airlee dead?" Edwin doesn't bother to conceal his concern.

"Yeah," Meyer says, "It's true. It's for the best. She was playing a game with a lot of bad men on her team. We took out one of their captains. It had to be done." He claps Edwin hard on the shoulder and continues to trudge down the hall, leaving him confused.

Airlee had only been dabbling when they first connected in the library. Since when was she ever a Rebel leader? There are only two leaders that he's even heard of – someone named

Zurie and a man who goes by many names. Some call him "the serpent."

Sanguine?

"What the Hell?" a guard screams from deep within the compound. The way the echo carries, it sounds like he's near the Sanitation Room. Guards scramble to get their gear and run to him. Edwin follows.

A black door – one everyone was told was sealed – hangs open, bent in on its hinges. The air that flows through smells fresher than they've ever smelled before, but the group doesn't dare step closer.

A tall man with a full, dark beard blocks the doorway, his hand on one hip and a dangerous smile on his maskless face.

"This isn't your supply entry," a skinny, blonde guard stammers from the back of the crowd.

"I was told you were a sad lot," the man's voice bellows, "but I wasn't expecting this." He scans the group, pausing on the skinniest and bloodiest men.

He steps to his right as more men filter through the doorway to stand behind him. Guns slung behind their shoulders and knives strapped to their waists, they don't move until their leader waves his hand forward.

The crowd surges away. The bearded man's soldiers pair up and push through them.

"Not one of you was man enough to so much as hit me," he shakes his head, "You truly are depressing. None of you will do." He brushes his hand over his facial hair.

Edwin's heart races. These aren't the Barclays. The same realization hits his fellow guards in roughly the same instant; they turn to run in a panic.

"My name is General Roclear, and I helped to win the War you lost. I know this is hard to believe, but you've been lied to all these years! You must now pay for your leader's mistakes. Sorry about that. I'll be taking twenty-five of you to sell to other compounds. We can do this the easy way, or we can do it the hard way."

He breezes through the hallway like he owns it.

Because he does.

Around the corner, Edwin watches as two men drag Amy, a mere teenage girl, down the hall. She screams like a wild animal in their arms. Her tiny voice quickly goes raw. Behind her, soldiers escort a little boy and someone he recognizes from the carpentry shop – he can't quite place the name, but the face is familiar enough.

It can't be true. These men must be cannibals, come to take them alive. Edwin doesn't know how they've managed to stay healthy without wearing gear – their own people have died within an hour of outdoor exposure even *with* masks – but he doesn't plan to visit their twisted society to find out how they do it.

Loud, high-pitched bangs come from the next hallway over. More screams erupt. Edwin backs away, breathless. His feet move without his permission, taking him far away from the noise in search of refuge.

Before he acknowledges what he's doing, his fist bangs on the door to Samuel's compartment.

No one answers. He pounds louder.

Finally, he hears movement from inside. He flinches when he sees Sam's face; he seems to have aged ten years overnight. Behind him, his home looks little more special than Edwin's own.

"We have to talk," Edwin rasps. The more he speaks, the more losing his voice becomes a problem.

"I figured," Sam gestures to the door. It occurs to Edwin that he probably woke him up.

"Men are in the building, taking people," Edwin breathes.

Samuel sighs. He knew the day would come when he'd have to explain the compound's dirtier truths, but he never expected that Edwin would be the first stranger to ask him. He hasn't prepared any kind of explanation.

Sam inhales slowly, hoping to calm himself down. It doesn't help. "The air is safe; this is something we've recently learned," he lies, "I don't think we can exactly go tanning, though. Prolonged exposure to the outdoors isn't likely to be safe."

"You didn't answer about the men."

"And I won't," Sam answers simply. Edwin just nods, knowing he won't get any further.

"Is it true, what you said about Airlee?" Edwin frowns.

Sam rubs his chin. "She's alive, but she'll be imprisoned for life. She wouldn't be alive if I had my way, but," he pauses, "marriage."

A long silence passes as Edwin cries tears of joy and confusion. One second dead, the next alive – but Sam would know. She's survived, after all!

With each second, Sam gradually breaks down. Not a single tear escapes his eyelids, but it's obvious that Edwin has pulled at a thread that threatens to completely unravel the fabric of Sam's existence. Sam chokes on his words as he tries to explain.

"We're not producing, Edwin. We might not get shipments soon, especially with this interruption. If that happens, we're dead. I don't know what to do to restore order. People may hate me, but even Alder doesn't have a clue what to do. Things have never been this bad."

Edwin keeps his eyes on his shoes.

"I need you to keep this a secret until I can clear the air myself, Edwin. Can you do that for me?"

He looks up. Sam might be right. There's no way he'll restore order and be able to keep people safe if they know the truth.

Sam pauses before re-entering his compartment. "River will be happy to hear you're okay."

The screams down the hall subside. A metallic clang echoes throughout – probably the hatch slamming shut. Sam snaps the lock to his compartment closed, waiting for the onslaught.

23 / SANGUINE

*H*e knows better than to hide away in his little room on the Most Privileged side. The Rebellion's plans are crude, but lengthy. The attack wasn't a spit and sit operation; there will be plenty more. Despite some small hiccups, everything had gone smoothly. With some luck, the next phase will go down without any kinks, too.

The supply closet reeks ironically of bleach and mold, a pretty solid indication that someone hasn't been doing their job, even with the tools mere inches away. Sanguine catches himself wishing that the lazy bastard would get caught, but stops himself as he remembers why he's in the closet to begin with.

Someone is cleaning house.

And beyond that, he isn't going to let Sam send him out for the Test; he doesn't know what will happen, but he knows that historically, he won't make it back alive.

Aside from the smell, the space doesn't bother him. It's the perfect spot to hide out in. Lengthy cracks make seeing through the door a breeze and voices seem to float right through, alerting him to passerby. Perhaps above everything, it's close to his target.

He plays with the sharp tip of his blade, an antique knife with a thick handle that seems to have gotten little use. In truth, his nerves are getting to him. His breath shakes, each exhalation fighting to break through the electricity in the air.

He's waited in the same spot for hours, watching people come and go, waiting for an opportunity. Any second, Sam will turn the corner, returning from the basement where he's surely told his wife that the invaders have gone. Sanguine will plunge the old knife into his back, hopefully piercing his heart cleanly.

At last, Sam arrives at the door to his little suite, a grey cloak poorly obscuring his identity. He fiddles with the keys in his pocket, every slow movement revealing his fatigue. He pauses before inserting the key into the lock and stares down at his hands, considering something – or perhaps nothing at all.

Sanguine turns the closet's old knob. He nudges the door forward and squeezes through the smallest opening, trying to minimize creaks and unwanted attention. He inhales deeply and exhales rapidly, not realizing that his breath is audible.

Samuel hears the anxious sounds of a man much bigger than himself hovering behind him; however, he doesn't turn around in time.

The knife plunges deep into Samuel's back. He gasps as it pierces his lung and grazes his heart. It dawns on Sanguine that Samuel will probably drown in his own blood. The death will be slow. He deserves the pain.

Red splatters the grubby white door as Samuel coughs. He claws at its hinges aimlessly in his struggle for breath, but Sanguine has him secured, his elbow crooked over his throat.

With a sudden twist of the knife, Sanguine cuts firmly into Samuel's heart. He falls to his knees and croaks as his vision becomes spotty. A part of him welcomes peace, *sleep at last*, but he fights unconsciousness, anyway. Even so, he fully blacks out within seconds. As soon as Sanguine lays him on the floor, a deep red puddle grows.

There's no way he can survive the blood loss alone.

The emptiness in the hallway envelops Sanguine like a warm blanket. He knows instantly that it was the wrong thing to do, and that he'd do it again.

24 / SANGUINE

Sanguine roams the hallways erratically after scrubbing the blood from his clothes using the bleach from the supply closet. *At least someone's putting it to use,* he thinks, but chides himself for making such trivial observations. He'd been smart enough to wear gloves, but there was more blood than he expected; it had streaked the bottoms of his sleeves and drizzled onto the hems of his pants. He's certain it's stuck to the soles of his boots, too.

Sleep commands most of his attention, but there's one more component to his plan he must complete before he'll let himself rest.

He has to show everyone that Sam lied. Airlee's alive.

He stomps his way to the makeshift jail River created for the girl. She'll hate him for releasing her – River has developed a soft spot for her – but so be it. They need to see. Everyone needs to see that she's alive and that they've been lied to.

It would be the icing on the cake after just being invaded. They'd revere him for presenting the truth. There couldn't be better timing, really; but who exactly were those soldiers? Were they who they said they were?

The hallways are eerily quiet, bridging into silence as he descends the concrete ramp into the basement. He sucks in a breath of chilly air as he prepares to face River. He'll get her riled up and probably send her on her way, too.

She's nowhere to be found. Good. He flows through the abandoned office, unlocks the door, and trudges to the end of the hall, where he collapses onto a shoddily made wooden bench. He sits for a moment with his eyes shut. Above him, the old fluorescent lights blink. Like so many other areas of the compound, the cellar bathes its inhabitants in a painfully dull yellow glow. The best lights in the place are in Luna Bay, but now they're probably wrecked somewhere among a pile of rubble. He shakes his head again.

A scuffing sound to his left rouses his attention. Airlee peeks her head out of the bars of a cell; someone must have locked her in. Her sunken, murky grey eyes cut into him.

He's surprised by the lack of anxiety he feels in her presence. They come from the same place. They share the same values.

"Don't worry," Sanguine stutters, "I haven't come to mercy

you."

Airlee makes a question mark with her hand.

"To free you," Sanguine answers, "But I want to talk to you first."

Airlee bolts upright as the building's alarm system goes off. She raises her hand in a question mark again.

He speaks, but she can't hear him over the alarms. She cuts him off by shaking her head and covering an ear with her hand. It's been so long since she's bathed that her palm sticks slightly to her skin.

He takes a moment to think about how to explain with his hands; the signs don't immediately come to him. Instead he points to her and then to his eyes as if to say *you will see.* He's used to watching people communicate and not reacting, him- self. Airlee sits crouched, ready to run if the need comes up. Something doesn't feel right.

Steps come from the hallway, the clack of heels echoing. A woman appears wearing a dull crimson pantsuit and brown boots; all worn down, yet still in fair enough shape to look good. Sanguine raises his eyebrows.

"You did it! You actually pulled off an attack," she shouts and raises her hands in the air. Even Airlee can hear her in her excitement, the alarms still blaring.

Sanguine's voice remains neutral even as his anxious

hands quake, but Airlee can barely hear him.

"Of course there was no other way," the blonde replies darkly and waits again for him to speak. The excitement has wiped clean from her face. He's told her something.

"Someone needed to do it, MacRose. I didn't see you offering. Sam is dead and I'm going to show everyone she's alive."

Airlee's head reels. MacRose? The Councilwoman?

"You're going to parade this girl around *now*? We need a morale boost. This will crush everyone. I can't let you do it."

He glares at her as she continues.

"I was interested, you know? Save our people. But if this is some sick power play..." she laughs and trails off. "How could I be so stupid? I didn't think you'd actually kill the guy. We met our goal; we proved Sam was full of shit and you offed him, anyway. I know this doesn't end with him."

Sanguine prays that if he ignores her, she'll go away.

He takes a key out of his pocket and twists it into the cell's lock. With a click, the door swings open. Airlee pokes her head timidly out. She moves into the hall and raises her eyes to Sanguine. *What is going on?*

"You," MacRose points at her, "Look, you can't listen to him. He's using you! He killed Sam; you can't trust a shitleaf like him."

Sanguine steps between them.

He turns and tucks a strand of dark hair behind Airlee's small ears, frowning at the thought of what he's about to do. He untucks the elastic of her mask and watches as it sinks to the floor. Underneath it, he finds a set of lips as pink as his own, differing only in the lines and scars from where hers were stitched together.

Airlee was born fully functional; it wasn't until her toddler years that her body was mutilated. She doesn't know this, but Sanguine does; he smuggled her medical records as soon as he heard she was imprisoned. Not only can he now prove she's alive, but he's got the proof of her surgery to back up his position on the compound.

Shame overwhelms her. She takes a step to the side and tips her chin down.

"You snake," MacRose murmurs, "You sneaking son of a bitch. You can't do this to a person."

"I didn't do this to her," he takes his mask off, smiles, and inches his way closer, "You did."

Airlee's eyes bug out of her skull as she kicks him in the shin. MacRose readies herself behind him. She's wanted to sock someone for years; all the better that it's this fool. She needs to relieve some stress.

Sanguine stares after Airlee as she backs away.

"Wait!"

MacRose takes advantage of Airlee's magnetic pull to side-step behind him. She closes her eyes tightly, bracing herself for her first physical assault. Her right fist collides with the side of Sanguine's head, knocking him off his feet and into the wall.

"Get up, you filthy bastard," she says, a victorious smile spreading across her face.

He sprawls out, more dazed than hurt.

"Run!" she instructs Airlee.

Airlee isn't sure where she can go, but her feet move, anyway.

"Come back!" Sanguine pleads, getting up.

"You made a huge mistake," MacRose seethes, her body poised, "I'm ashamed you ever got me to believe in you."

His eyebrows nearly cross. He doesn't understand how anyone could still believe in Sam after those men barged in and took their people. He explains as much.

"He was just one man among monsters. None of us knows the truth. You killed the one person who knew."

"Tell River that."

"You really are stupid, aren't you?" she begins, "We pretend to hate each other so no one knows we're friends. I know *everything,* including who those men were. She had to tell someone in case anything happened to her and Sam."

He shakes his head. "Some friend you are, getting excited about cracking skulls your best friend has to put back together."

From her boot lining she draws a switchblade; she's not waiting on someone else to decide on this creep's fate. Sanguine grips his baton with a sweaty palm and takes a step back. MacRose leaps on him before he can even swing his weapon back.

25 / AIRLEE

The stale smell of Sanguine's body odor hits Airlee about the same time the severity of the situation does; something serious has happened, something bigger than her, something bigger than the Council. Things have spun out of control. She cringes. This might not just be a chance to frolic around the compound one last time; this might be her only real chance to escape. She glances at her facemask lying by the two pairs of rapidly moving feet.

If she goes with Sanguine and his plan works, he could be her master. She will always owe him. He seemed nice enough when she first met him, but now the thirst for power and validation sit heavy in his eyes.

She sprints in the other direction, never looking back. The corridor splits; *left, or right?* She follows the path she saw the butterfly emerge from, not quite knowing what to expect, but going for it, anyway.

Several doorways line the hall, most rooms locked and abandoned. The windows are caked with decades of dust, but some are clean enough to see through, revealing piles of toppled furniture. These rooms offer nothing to her. She peers down the remainder of the hall. Two bright blue butterflies and a dragonfly flutter by a large door at the dead end. Airlee doubles her efforts as soon as she sees the insects, but it's hard to move her stiff limbs as quickly as she'd like.

Her progress hits a wall as the compound's lights go out, leaving her in pitch-black darkness. She gropes around trying different doors she remembers seeing.

Before the lights blinked out, she saw an ancient red box hanging chest-height on a wall, the paint bubbled off in flecks on the floor. She heads in that direction, hugging the wall for guidance. As she nears the end of the hallway, she doesn't need to guess about the box's location anymore; a sliver of light from the door exposes its contents. In fact, everything is becoming easier to see.

Airlee dashes to the door. It's open about three inches, but locked by a thick, corroded metal chain. Faint screams fan through the basement. Whatever Airlee does, she must hurry. She retreats from the door only to rush at it, hoping to break the chain with body force alone.

The chain sustains no damage. She turns her head to the

red box and leaps to it across the dark. She shoves her elbow into the glass, freeing the old axe. It feels foreign to hold a weapon in her hands, a far cry from wooden dolls and chairs. She considers returning to the fight to prevent MacRose and Sanguine from killing each other, but sprints back to the door instead. Let them keep each other busy. Using all of her power, she slams the axe down on a particularly weak part of the chain, breaking one side of the link. One more blow, and the chain falls to the floor with a heavy thud.

"Airlee!" Sanguine calls from down the hall, his voice urgent and closer now.

She bends down to pick up the chain. With any luck, Sanguine won't see her silhouette through the dark. Without luck, he will attack – probably try to knock her out – but with a chain around her neck and an axe, will he really risk dying for her?

Yes, she thinks. *He would.*

And she would swing deep into his flesh to protect herself if it came down to it. She has no side. She knows this now – she just has to get out. They're *all* crazy.

She shakes the door open.

Machinery takes up most of the circular room, little bugs and cobwebs filling the empty spaces. It reeks of rust. *No wonder the air is terrible in this place,* she thinks, *if this is the main air filter, it's in terrible shape.* As she continues her brief exploration, she spots a damaged portion of the wall, chipped cement blocks and bricks scattered all over the floor. She looks back up to the air filter; small punctures mar its surface. It looks like something blew up nearby.

So, this is why the alarms went off. She thinks she can hear faint screams through the damaged part of the wall, but she doesn't stick around to evaluate any further.

A square line of light shines from the ceiling. A lengthy ladder runs down from it. She bounds for the rickety aluminum rungs and climbs as fast as she can to what she prays is a hatch of some kind; her distance vision has always been a little foggy.

"Airlee, where are you?" Sanguine screams, his voice cracking. He's halfway down the hall, about to step in thick shards of glass that will clue him in to Airlee's whereabouts.

She feels a glimmer of regret; axe and chain in hand, perhaps she should have intervened and prevented someone from getting hurt.

How would he even parade me around the compound? He tried to assassinate a councilor. Everyone must be looking for him.

Eyes on the hatch, Airlee continues ascending the ladder, not even stopping when it wobbles. As she reaches the same height as more severe damage on the wall, she's certain that the screams are not her imagination. She struggles to keep her movements quiet even though she knows that Sanguine will figure her out.

The old hatch rests a mere five feet away. Fresh air leaks through cracks in its lining. Airlee has to stop for a moment; the activity on her weary body, along with the change in air, makes her dizzy. She hugs the ladder for support, closes her eyes, and rests her head on a rung. A minute goes by before she musters the courage to crack open the hatch.

She hears a bang below her, but she doesn't pause to look.

She places her hands around the cold, rusty wheel and turns with all of her strength. Flakes of rust scrape off into her eyes.

The sounds of birds chirping flow through her ears; their lively melodies motivate her to keep going. She thrusts upward and the hatch bangs open. Airlee covers her eyes frantically and winces. So much sunlight pours over her, it's absolutely blinding.

The noises of the real world are intoxicating this time around; birds, wind, frogs, things she has no name for.

The ladder vibrates from beneath. Someone's quick steps follow her up.

26 / RIVER

River hovers over her husband, his skin already turning a grotesque shade of blue – his spirit gone, and only a body remaining. Tears spill over her eyelashes. Perhaps she and Samuel weren't the ideal match at times – they'd fought, they'd disagreed profoundly on moral issues – but they'd loved each other fiercely. She imagined growing old with him, sharing the same uncomfortable, bowing mattress, for many more years to come.

Now I'll grow old all alone.

She wonders where his soul has traveled, refusing to believe that his existence can altogether disappear. Perhaps one day they'll meet again.

A pang of guilt hits her in the stomach as another emotion surprises her: relief. She'll be able to handle the compound in her own way now, assuming the people accept her leadership.

The bloodstains on the floor in front of their compartment

will never truly disappear. Every time she unlocks this door, she'll be reminded of Sam's assassination.

If she had gone with him to their compartment when he let her know it was safe to leave the basement, he might still be alive. Or she might be dead. The newest strike began in the lab, no casualties but a few stem cells and some medicine.

It all interests her; some guards fight for the workers and some workers defend the guards. Everywhere, people accidentally kill their own simply because they don't know who is on their side and who isn't. All in all, everyone is simply destroying their own community. Putting themselves on equal terms — the Least Privileged putting aside their victimhood and the Most Privileged forgetting their biases — and talking about the issues and possible resolutions just wouldn't be gratifying enough. Not like this. Nothing is as gratifying as breaking things and grinding them down into nothing.

Part of the allure of that is rebirth, she knows, but she doesn't see how it's possible now.

When she saw Samuel's body, she didn't even bother to scream. She'd come to persuade him to do something, but from the moment she left her post, a boulder weighed her stomach down. Now, she can't even remember what it was she'd wanted him to do — have the medical officer inspect Airlee, maybe. Her wounds had the potential to get infected.

She should have expected someone to act aggressively. They should have planned for this. She clutches at the hole in his chest.

River doesn't bother to turn around at the hurried patter of footsteps behind her. If her husband's assailant wanted to do her in, as well, so be it.

"River, is that you?" Edwin asks, a trace of his lisp back.

She looks down at her knees, her clothing soaked in tepid blood. This is the last time his touch will ever feel warm. It's this that spawns the tears that blind her. She leans over his body and cries.

"I'm not gonna hurt you," Edwin reassures her. He crouches down and clasps a hand on her shoulder for a few seconds. "That medical officer is still here," Edwin says, "He can help you."

She grimaces. They don't have the supplies to bring him back. Depending on what's wrong, it might not even be possible even if they did have the necessities.

She rises from her knees and looks down on him. Months ago, she never thought they would be in this kind of situation together.

"I know you're not going to hurt me, Edwin," she says, beautiful even with a tear-streaked face. "Will you go somewhere with me?"

He nods.

"We're going to find Dr. Hasek."

If the Barclays aren't who they say they are, she thinks, *neither are you.*

It doesn't take the pair long – Hasek has stuck around to tend to victims. Unknown to them, he'd much rather save lives than deal with simple cases of toe fungus and digits lopped off during bad games of pin finger back at home. They explain the situation to him as they return to the body.

"I may be able to bring him back," Hasek states, "but he's lost a lot of blood. Have the hoodlums left the laboratory?"

River nods enthusiastically.

"Grab a blanket. We'll lift him onto it and take him there," Hasek says.

She returns with the thickest blanket in the compartment. It takes all three of them to lift him into it.

"His blood type?"

"AB, I think," River answers.

"'I think' will have to do," Hasek huffs as they get moving, "You've got blood. I took stock of it."

In what seems like an instant, they reach the lab. The blanket – Sam's favorite – is soaked through with blood. The feeling drains out of her hands as she watches the doctor prepare him on the table; cutting open his most comfortable shirt, hooking him up to receive blood. Even though Sam's already gone, she can't help but want to yell at Hasek for destroying his clothes. What will he wear to stay cozy when this nightmare is all over? Her face turns red thinking about it. She watches as he inspects the wound and shakes his head.

"Son, take her out of here. You *both* still have people to help," Hasek murmurs, "River, you don't need to see the rest of this. I don't think I can bring him back, but I'm going to try."

"Why?"

Her question catches him off-guard. "Pardon?"

"You aren't with the Barclays. You're with *them*. Why help us?"

He focuses on the wound and clamps it open. River cringes. *That must hurt*, she thinks. Then she remembers he's already dead. Hasek reaches for a cauterizer.

"I mean it when I say you should leave, but if you need to know, I work here because I'm told to. Everything else is because I believe people are people. Doesn't matter who won or lost the War. Now, please, get out." His head snaps up.

She watches him operate while Edwin gently pulls her out of the room.

"What are we going to do?" River asks no one in particular.

"Have faith. He's skilled," Edwin soothes. It doesn't help.

River knows it's over. The blood has begun to dry on her fore-arms. Her body shakes.

They stand for a moment in silence, River an impulse away from snapping the door back open.

His focus averts. "I know who did this and it's my fault. I don't deserve to be here."

"No," she cups his chin in one graceful motion, "You don't deserve to be here. Come with me."

Her weary eyes droop. Physical exertion, emotional exhaustion, and a lack of sleep threaten her senses. She wanders the halls without paying attention to others, Edwin following in her wake. She's not the only one on autopilot.

Workers sign to each other: *They have fresh food in storage. Look at all these shower stalls! There's so much blood – should we help?* Most just stand around, unsure of themselves.

Margeaux, standing along a wall, watches the pair go by. With nothing better to do she joins them, keeping a safe distance. In the mess of the crowds, they don't register her behind them.

River and Edwin ascend some steps in an abandoned part of the compound, its entrance taped off. The stairway is dark, its only windows resting adjacent to the ceiling and painted over. At the top of the stairs, she presses her foot against a two-inch block sticking from the wall. The pressure from her leg triggers a hidden door to open, revealing yet another. River fishes from her large key ring and unlocks it.

"Sam told me about this just a couple of nights ago," she whispers, "Please use it. If not now, later."

She glances at him and then at the door. It's time someone else knows the facts about the compound before all of its secrets die with their keepers. She hasn't heard from Alder or MacRose. For all she knows, they're dead, too. The secret is too critical to keep to themselves now.

"It leads outside, Edwin. There's a vent through this door – worn out to uselessness, if I have the right one. We filtered air from it – and many others – to provide safe oxygen for us to breathe."

"Samuel told me the air is mostly okay now," Edwin says, searching her distracted eyes.

River frowns. "For now, it is, but everyone here is tired. We're going to starve and keep being taken away. We have no choice but to live a harsh life. Out there, maybe you'll have true freedom," she pauses. "Do you remember the story of the War? How people stayed inside for years? That's the only true part of the story. We lost. Those men are our captors."

Edwin doesn't know what to say to her; she must be delirious.

Tears flood her eyes again. She clasps his hands. "Sam told me something you may not want to hear... We lost the War, Edwin. A long time ago. We're slaves. They found our hubs and safe zones and took everything over. They're out there now, doing whatever they want, while we toil away and tear each other apart. Our only hope is to assimilate somewhere less harsh."

"I don't understand," Edwin backs away, "The Barclays won the War?"

"No, Edwin. The Triune did. Specifically, the Federacy rules here. The Barclays have always been the Federacy. Everything we say we've been trading to help the United Army is really for the enemy. I'm so sorry."

"How many are there?" Edwin steps forward.

"There's a city near here. There are thousands of them – who knows how many elsewhere? Sam told me they guard places like ours. It's why our air quality testers really never come back. They shoot them."

Edwin glares. "And Sam still sends people out?"

"The Federacy mandates it. The tests seemed to give people hope, something to look forward to. It makes them more productive."

Edwin's eyes narrow. "And the mutations?"

"A control device. Mostly."

Edwin's heart thumps madly until it feels like it will burst from his chest. He knows what he wants before she even offers the option to him.

"I'm not asking anything," she says, "I'm leaving it up to you. You can start over. Maybe you can bring us help, or there's someone out there we don't know about. You can leave now or tell everyone you know about this exit or you can stay here and see this through. I'm leaving it up to you."

"What about you?" Edwin asks.

"I haven't decided yet," she lies.

"Can I see it first?" he asks shyly.

She doesn't respond, just merely steps toward the door and opens it to reveal a little room with a tank on one wall. A battered aluminum vent with an attached hose faces the door, sunlight creeping through slits and cracks. River pries the vent off with her bare hands and tosses it onto the floor, the piece making a sickening metallic clang. Despite being five feet tall, it doesn't weigh much. At this moment, Edwin turns back to face the door. The lights in the stairwell have gone out.

River pauses. The next layer she must remove is a thick piece of foam. It smells medicated somehow despite showing signs of molding. She looks at Edwin, urging him with her expression to do the rest of the job himself.

He pulls tenderly at the foam's edges, soon realizing it

needs a solid yank to give way. He rips it from its position, tearing the material in the most worn out places. River sighs from behind him, the weight of her impulsive decision bearing down on her – even though it's the right one.

The foam leaves a thick cloud of dust in the air, making her sneeze. At last, Edwin removes the final shred of foam, illuminating the room in a kind of natural light that neither of them has ever seen before. The dust, they can now see, floats around the room like glitter. One more metallic vent blocks them from a bright, big world.

"What in the Hell is this?" a familiar voice roars from behind them. His wildly contorted face points in River's direction.

"What in the Hell is *this*? *Why* are you following us when people need you?" River cries, her entire body tensing up. "My *husband* needed you."

"You'll kill us all!" Meyer yells. "We've already been contaminated!"

"Let me explain–" River starts, but he doesn't acknowledge her.

"The way you killed Airlee, or quicker?" Edwin glares. He regrets ever saving the liar.

"I didn't kill Airlee personally," Meyer replies, "But I will kill you." He lunges at the pair, revealing Margeaux's shadowy figure standing behind him. River stares with her mouth open, immobile.

Margeaux yanks his arm to the left, knocking him off balance. He whips around to face her.

An old, splintery plank of wood rests on the wall near Edwin, smothered in cobwebs. He grabs for it silently, reaches his arms back, and smashes it against Meyer's head just a second before he reaches Margeaux. The board breaks in half. Meyer crumples at River's feet.

They exhale in relief simultaneously as they stare dumbfounded at Margeaux standing in the doorway.

Margeaux makes walking motions with her fingers and shrugs. She raises a hand at Edwin in a question mark, points at him, and signs the name "Zurie."

Why are you with Zurie?

River looks to Edwin for translation.

"You gotta be kidding. She followed us," Edwin begins, pausing as Margeaux nods and covers her fingers with her other hand, "She must've hid under the stairs." She cups her hand behind her ear and rocks it back and forth. "She heard everything." He pauses, not knowing how to continue. "You're Zurie, River? All of this was you?" He looks like he could cry.

"I... I wanted change. The Rebellion broke into factions. The more desperate we got, the more people fled to violence. A guard named Sanguine did this. Not me. Margeaux reached out to me after Airlee was taken. That's how she knows who I am."

Margeaux looks to the prone body sprawled on the floor. She makes a slicing motion with one finger against her neck, followed by a question mark.

"If he's not dead, he's out of it for a while," River reassures her. "Thank you for distracting him." She bends down and checks his neck for a pulse, just to be sure – nothing. "He's gone," she says. One more name to add to the list of the deceased.

Edwin's blood boils. He wants to cry from the sheer stress of the last few months, but holds off. The faster he can have some peace alone, the better. In one swift motion, he kicks open the vent.

Light spills out of the little exit, bathing the room in a brilliant glow. The warmth of sunshine washes over them like water from a faucet. Not one of them has seen sunlight like this before. They take a moment to adjust to it. In a minute, they can see white clouds swimming in the ocean of blue sky above them.

River is the first to step outside of the compound. Dry dirt swirls around her feet. She sucks in a breath of fresh summer air and watches the birds flit back and forth between trees, singing songs of joy. A red squirrel leaps from branch to branch, playing with another creature River cannot see. She's tempted to walk around the area and allow the long, untouched grass to tickle her legs and hips, but all at once, she feels she doesn't deserve this beauty.

She is also overcome by fear; the place is guarded, but no one knows how well, or where the soldiers watch.

Edwin pops his head out of the exit, his salt and pepper hair shining in the natural sunlight. Panic strikes him as he remembers nightmares of doing exactly this, his body melting apart, but he's soon distracted. His eyes can't focus in one direction. A slight breeze flows through the air from the north, giving him his first taste of a cooling summer wind. The birds, the squirrels, the bright blue sky and emerald green grass... The sensations terrify and enliven him. He moves out of the room and takes his first steps on real land.

Ahead of him, the grass sways with sudden movement. A little black animal bounds out of the weeds and gracefully stops in front of the pair to announce itself with a lovely little call. Its tail flicks through the air and it scampers away, meowing aimlessly. Its voice floats away in the wind.

River looks back inside the room, only to find that a green filter obscures her vision as she stares into the darkness. "Are you coming out?" she calls.

Margeaux steps into the doorway, but doesn't step out. She flinches at the light as it floods her vision. From left to right she turns, not particularly blown away. Someone like her wouldn't survive in the wild – that alone makes the natural world difficult for her to appreciate. Margeaux shakes her head and points to herself and back at the compound, signaling that she wants to stay to see how things play out.

"Good luck, Margeaux. If you don't mind exploring the basement, Airlee is there. She has some kind of dog with her," River says, "May peace be with you."

Margeaux waves at Edwin and returns the way she came. She stands a little straighter. New life has sprung into her step. Despite her circumstances, she'll be back.

"What happened to Airlee?" Edwin asks, searching River's face. Outside, her pale skin glows and her eyes light up in a way that Edwin has never seen before. Her tired face is beautiful, but he sees the deadly metamorphoses of her expressions. Someone will have to pay. He hopes she doesn't end up making herself do it.

"Samuel locked her up and planned on killing her," she explains, "At least, at first. I convinced him to keep her a prisoner for the time being. Her 'death' was supposed to ruin morale – numb the Rebellion."

Edwin mulls over this information and takes a few steps

closer to the grass. He moves his eyes skyward – his first time ever studying the clouds. One floats high above the compound in the shape of an elephant, its trunk extended.

The compound itself is much smaller than either of them realized; it's nothing more than an abandoned two-floor warehouse, the windows of the second floor shattered in several spots.

"Someone built an underground bunker. They knew something bad was coming," Edwin says. River nods.

He focuses in on a vibrant yellow flower by the corner of the building. Although he has no name for it, it's a dandelion, and he thinks it's beautiful. He spots several patches of them growing undeterred.

"If I let you go, you'll die," River places a hand on his shoulder. "You could stay."

"If I stay, I'm already dead."

In the distance, he spots a woman walking uphill through a patch of tall wildflowers. Edwin is sure it's Airlee, the trim outline of her body familiar. Sanguine trails behind, limping in her wake. She looks over her shoulder and picks up her pace, making it clear she's trying to escape him. Edwin's leftover reservations evaporate.

River stares out at the duo. *Is Airlee holding an axe?* Her lips strain into a thin line.

"What's the point of living if you're only staying alive?" Edwin frowns. "Thank you, River. For being kind."

"I'm being human," she replies.

"Humans aren't kind. You're special."

"Maybe in another life I was something better. But not this one. Goodbye, Edwin."

So much loss. She's not sure what to do with herself.

He nods his head and runs in Airlee's direction, leaving River to make her own decision privately. She watches as he parts overgrown weeds, his overworked fingers lingering on the prickly plants. He disappears down a small hill as he slows to admire a few Moonwalker sunflowers.

River holds her breath; it's as if he's been plucked out of thin air. She breathes again as she catches sight of him hurrying uphill.

If she returns and things stabilize, she'll do no more than go through the motions, simply existing, waiting for something exciting to happen to her. When something does happen, it's bound to be negative. *I'll probably die if I'm being honest with myself.* If she can find a new home for her people or someone willing to side with them against the Federacy, there might be hope.

No one will benefit from her sitting in solitude and mourning Sam.

She walks the perimeter of the building and finds others escaping from various spots.

Dr. Hasek. He would know the exits well enough to show them to people. His final act of care. She spots him at the edge of the building, directing people away from the east. "Hey!" she yells.

Several heads turn in her direction; one of them is Hasek's. His eyes meet hers languidly. With a shake of his head, he confirms the worst without even speaking a word. Unable to hold her gaze, he turns around and goes back to work.

The heat of the summer sun makes River's dehydrated body dizzy, but no one notices her in their wonderment. She doesn't care about any of it – the sun, the sky, the green grass small animals scamper around on. The compound was her world. Sam was her world. She doesn't know anything about this new one. Her mouth is so dry she feels like she could choke.

She considers following Sanguine and giving him what he deserves, but thinks better of it; killing him won't have any positive impact on her life. It's far too late. If their paths cross again, she'll think differently, but she can't let herself get dragged into more carnage now. She must focus on finding help for her people.

She lets him go, fully accepting that what she'll do to him

when she finds him will fundamentally change who she is as a person. For now, though, she still has people to protect. Workers don't venture too far from the building, their dependence on it acting as ball and chain.

Maybe the trio will find help headed north. River heads south alone to tread more ground, leaving her whole world and everyone she knows behind. With luck, she'll return soon with good news.

She knows that tonight when she's alone and trying to sleep, the positivity will fade. She will miss Sam and pine for the old life; but for now, the future is open. So long as she doesn't get shot.

The black creature darts in front of her, brushing against her legs.

"Hi, kitty," she says, reaching down to pet the animal's soft fur. It purrs at her gentle touch.

The cat walks beside her as she begins her trek through overgrown woods and onto an abandoned trail. The cat meows at her, twirling its tail around her leg. Her little green eyes contain more life than most people's she's seen.

The animal gives her hope, but she doesn't know why. The wild thing at her feet knows more about how to live happily than humans ever will.

A shot echoes from within the eastern forest. River picks

up her pace, wishing now that she hadn't chosen to go alone. Birds scatter from the trees.

www.ingramcontent.com/pod-product-compliance
Lightning Source LLC
Chambersburg PA
CBHW031228120726
47905CB00002B/512